Marti Talbott's Highlander Series

Book 5

(Clare, Dolee, Catlin & Lasha)

By

Marti Talbott

-

Editor: *Frankie Sutton*

NOTE: All of Marti Talbott's Books are suitable for young adults 14 and older. Sign up to be notified when new books are published at martitalbott.com

CLARE

CHAPTER I

In the Month of April, on the eighth day, in the year of our Lord 11—

My Beloved Clare,

I cannot seem to think of anything but you, yet I am aware of your caution not to write so often for fear you will be punished. I cannot bear the thought of that happening on my account. Just know my heart is constantly with you.

Father is gravely ill yet he lingers and suffers, which I would not wish upon anyone. He is a good man, mostly, but set in the ways of passing the inheritance to a son who marries according to his father's wishes.

I do so hope you are understanding of my position. As you are well aware, without the inheritance I would have no way of caring for you.

Would that I could, I would this very day carry you away and keep you in my arms forever

Soon, my love, soon.

Alcott of Cumberland

The adjustment from a well-regimented life in an Abbey, to complete freedom in the MacGreagor Clan made Clare feel lost and ill at ease. Before long she was driving her sister daft asking for permission to do this or that, but a lifetime of habits die hard. Thankfully, Greer was very understanding.

Even more overwhelming was the sudden attention of so many men. More than one MacGreagor learned the words in English and mentioned her extraordinary beauty, but it was not a welcome compliment. Attractiveness, she learned early on in life, was more of a curse than an asset. While she was carefully watched and surrounded by other women in the Abbey, there were occasions when a man in their company wanted her in his bed.

However, none did not, indeed could not, offer marriage. Some men in authority taught self-denial but did not always practice it and when she declined, which she repeatedly did, she was given the hardest of all chores. Therefore, Clare's plight in life was to keep weeds out of the rows and rows of vegetable and herb gardens.

Working outside caused problems when visitors came and occasionally a man would offer to pay for her attentions and even her freedom. It was then the priests decided she should dress in the clothing of a monk with a hood to hide her comeliness. She did not mind, the hood protected her from the sun and more often than not she enjoyed the extra warmth.

Daily she prayed for Greer to fetch her -- nightly she went to bed in the room filled with dedicated nuns and tried not to let her heart hurt too badly. Then something extraordinary happened -- she was allowed to go to market with Marlow for the first time ever and it was there she met him.

Alcott of Cumberland had eyes so brown they were nearly black and the color of his hair matched them. So mesmerizing were his features, she could not later remember what he wore, other than it was a blue tunic with white trim. Perhaps he wore a crest denoting his station in life but she could not recall.

Had he asked, she would have gone anywhere with him, but he did not ask and, because of the clerics and the wall around the Abbey, it was the only time she ever saw him up close.

Conditions were complicated on both sides and all they had of each other was a meager exchange of letters. Then word came that Alcott of Cumberland was dead and Clare was devastated.

The very next day, four enormous Highlanders brought her sister, Greer, inside the wall of the Abbey and Clare was saved. Her grief and her joy were so overwhelming, she hardly noticed the journey into Scotland, nor did she mind so much that she had no clothing save the boring brown she wore under the brown robe with a hood.

Once they finally reached the rest of the clan in Northern Scotland, she was given a hot bath in the chambers of Mistress Glenna, the clothing of the MacGreagors and allowed to unbraid and brush her beautiful, long, golden hair.

She was home.

"Home," Clare whispered. Seated at the small table in the cottage she shared with Greer, she pondered exactly what the word meant. Sent to the clerics at the age of five, she hardly remembered living in the home of her parents, and although the parents managed to visit them once a year, she and Greer were never taken back home even for a holiday. She had, or so she was told, two elder brothers and three elder sisters. Clare and her sister were simply two daughters too many and she tried not to think that her parents bribed the clerics to take her. But with the gifts of jewels and farm animals they gladly gave, what else could it have been?

When the door opened, Clare quickly covered her glower with a smile, a trait she learned out of necessity in her youth. "Sister, you have come back for something?"

A tall woman with Clare's same blond hair and soft blue eyes, Greer instantly began to fan herself with her hand, "Good heavens, you will cook if you stay inside in this heat."

It was hot. Clare tried leaving the door open earlier, but people...mostly men... kept coming to the door asking if she were unwell. She was quite well, she just wanted a wee bit of solitude. "Is it always this hot in the Highlands?"

"They say this is very rare and I believe it. Usually it is cloudy and because I love the sunshine, we must enjoy it while we can. I insist you come for a walk with me."

These days, Greer was always happy and it had a great deal to do with a certain Highlander by the name of Brendan. Once she finally let herself, she fell completely and madly in love with him and soon they would marry -- that is, as soon as Clare adjusted and was able to get on by herself.

*

The unusual heat drove all the people outside, even Laird Neil MacGreagor, who was sitting on a short rock wall in the courtyard. The three story keep he called home offered some shade as did nearby trees, although most trees had long since been cleared away to make room for cottages. Meandering paths connected both old and new cottages surrounding the Keep, a river marked the clan's border to the north and a lush, wide glen to the south held their herds of horses, cattle and sheep.

Normally surrounded by men, this day was no exception and Laird Neil MacGreagor found himself giving fewer orders, since most of the harder labors could be put off for a cooler day. The women congregated on the opposite side of the courtyard, and sat in chairs under the shade of the trees, fussing with sewing or just watching the children play. The boys, Neil's son Justin included, played a game flicking small stones at other small stones, trying to force them over a line drawn in the dirt. Little girls stayed closer to their mothers and pretended they were queens, while babies slept in wooden boxes.

But when Greer and Clare walked by, the men could not seem to help themselves. Several stopped in mid-sentence and gawked at Clare's beauty. The women, on the other hand, watched the besotted men and then glared until the men noticed. More than one guilty husband quickly came to kiss his wife and reassure her, but those who did not take the trouble were sure to face intense discussions later.

CHAPTER II

Greer looped her arm through her sister's, and waited until they were down the path between the newer cottages and could not be overheard. "The lads want to know what they must do to get your notice."

Clare took a deep breath and let it out. "I did not come here to marry, I came to escape the Abbey and be with you. Let them marry the ones who are willing."

"You do not intend to take a husband?"

"Not now and perhaps not ever. Besides, I have nothing to offer a husband. All I know how to do is weed gardens and the lads do that here."

"I thought you hated weeding gardens."

"I surely do, but I know nothing else. I am not a weaver, I do not know how to sew or cook, or even wash clothes. My punishment was the gardens."

"Punishment?"

"I would not consent, you see."

"Oh, I do see." Greer stopped them for just a moment before they started into the pastures. "Watch where you walk. Nothing is more unpleasant than to get droppings on your shoes. I should know I have stepped in it often enough." She enjoyed a rare smile from her sister and started them walking again. "What kind of life did you dream of before you left the Abbey?"

"Mostly, the kind a woman like me cannot have. I never truly believed I would leave the Abbey so I tried not to dream. And I must confess, life in the Highlands never crossed my mind."

Greer stopped walking and turned her sister to face the highest hill. "I want to climb that hill but if we try, a dozen lads will come to protect us."

"Only a dozen? I am appalled."

Greer giggled. "Perhaps we might outrun them and get away before they catch up."

"Run...uphill? The heat has addled your brain."

"In that case, we will try it on a cooler day. What I mean to say is...avoiding lads no matter where one goes is impossible. They are everywhere and they want to be near you. It is not wrong of them; it is the way of lads and lasses."

"I know you are right, it is just that I am not ready. I want to learn to breathe first, to come and go without permission and to enjoy my freedom."

"And you fear a husband would take your freedom away?"

Clare closed her eyes and nodded. "You do understand."

"Of course I do, I lived in the Abbey for a time too."

"It is not her fault she is bonnie." Seated on the grass several feet away from the others in the courtyard, Dora absentmindedly played with the end of her braided red hair, and watched Glenna put Ceanna over her shoulder and begin to pat the baby's back.

Dora was the first of the English dairy maids to consent to become a bride in Scotland just a few short weeks ago. Neither she nor Carol had settled on a man, nor had any of the men settled on them. For a time, Dora thought Moan preferred her and then there were others who caught her eye, but although they were pleasant enough, none seemed to develop into an attachment. The language barrier made it too hard to communicate.

Dora was not alone. Most of the over fifty women brought from England were still trying to learn enough Gaelic and had not chosen husbands. Neil feared those who had, chose too quickly and declared all weddings postponed for a time.

It seemed to Carol the heat made everyone ill-tempered, although she believed she was handling it better than most. Still, she could not help complaining on this one particular subject. "But did you see how Clare walked in front of all the lads?"

"Where would you have her walk? Should she go all the way around the village to get to the other side? Even then, lads would still turn to watch her," said Dora.

"Then the lads should be told not to look at her."

"If a lad does not look, I would think him near death. Even Neil looked."

Carol drew in a sharp breath, "Did his wife notice."

"I do not know, but I imagine there is little Glenna does not notice."

"She does not look upset." Carol glanced at the faces of some of the other married women to see if they were upset. Some did not look happy. "Dora, if we do not do something about Clare, the rest of us are not likely to have a husband. They all want her."

"Do something about Clare? What are you suggesting?"

Carol stood up and brushed off the back of her skirt. Her blond hair was long enough to braid and then tie in a knot on top of her head to keep it off her neck. The braid made a loop some of the other women found delightful and tried to imitate. "I am not suggesting anything. I am just saying I liked it much better when Clare hid behind that brown hood." She turned and headed back to the river where she believed the air was cooler.

*

As they usually did, the men who kept watch on the outskirts of their land in the daytime, exchanged places with the night guards and returned home late in the afternoon. Almost always they had at least some snippets of gossip gathered from other clans passing through the land. It was Tristan who rode into the courtyard, quickly dismounted and went to give Neil the news. Intentionally, he kept his voice low hoping not to upset the women.

"Slain?" Neil could hardly believe his ears and he too kept his voice low, which caused the men to move in closer and the women's ears to perk up.

"Three executioners," Tristan continued. "The newly crowned king has vowed to expose the lads responsible, but most believe the new king himself is responsible."

"So it begins," Neil muttered.

"Aye, the English are beside themselves with grief over the loss of their beloved king, and they greatly fear the new one. They say it is George of Leics. Scotland's king left straight away from his residence in the south to the one in the north. It is said he did not even wait for his wife and children to make ready before he and his guard rode swiftly away. What do you think it means, Neil?"

"It means we got out of England with the brides just in time, and life is about to change for all of us. Walrick, tomorrow you and Brendan will ride to Laird MacPhearson and ask what he has heard. Ask to see his dragon and he will know I sent you."

"Done," said Walrick. He quickly got up from his seat on the wall and went off to find Brendan.

Neil then turned to Gelson. "Take Burk and ask the same of Laird Graham." He waited for Gelson's nod and then turned back to the guard. "You have done well. Find Luag and send him to me, then go to your rest."

As soon as Tristan was gone, Neil walked across the courtyard to his wife, bent down and kissed Glenna's forehead. Then he took the baby out of her arms and cradled her. "I see you are eating well, my little love. You will soon be too heavy for even me." He smiled at the baby's gurgle.

"Husband, has the guard brought unhappy news?"

Neil glanced at all the women watching and waiting for his response. "Unfortunately, it *is* unhappy news. The king of England was murdered."

Glenna could not help but bring her hand up to cover her gasp. "I must tell Jessup."

"Aye. Tell her I would like a word with her when she is able. And see if you can get her to let the lads take her bed outside. It cannot be good for her or the baby to be inside in this heat."

"I will convince her." Glenna put her cheek next to his, lovingly touched her daughter's hair and then motioned for two men to come with her.

*

What Jessup MacGreagor, beloved friend to the slain Kind of England, did not need, was more bad news and her loudly complaining baby was just as unhappy.

It was customary for a woman to stay in bed for weeks after giving birth, and most women were unhappy with the condition after only a few days. But the fear of losing a wife drove the men to insist upon it. So when Glenna knocked on the door, she was not surprised that Lucas opened it.

She smiled, went in and looked at her friend. "Just as I thought, you are red in the face from this heat and the child is too hot as well." She took the baby out of his box, walked to the door and held it open so the breeze could cool him. "Lucas, if you will lift your wife, the lads will take her bed outside."

Lucas was more than happy to oblige. The sweat was pouring off of him too, but when he reached for her, Jessup glared. "I am quite capable of walking."

"You are quite capable of stubbornness too. However, I will agree to anything to get out of this heat."

Jessup slipped her legs over the side of the bed, took his hand and stood up. Then she stepped out of the way while the two men came in and moved her bed outside. "Glenna, nothing we do calms our son, what can be the matter with him? And do not say the heat. He has been distressed since he was born."

Glenna felt his hard stomach and nodded. "I will show you a trick my mother used for her eight upset babies." She followed Jessup out, waited for her to lie back down, and then nodded her appreciation to Lucas for bringing out two chairs and putting them in the shade next to the bed.

Once they were all settled, she turned the baby over and put him face down across her lap. "When mothers are upset, the baby gets upset too, or so I have been told. However, my mother claimed she was never upset, so who knows if it is true. At any rate, Lucas will want to learn her trick as well, for I do not have good news."

"What?" Jessup reluctantly asked.

Carefully, Glenna put one hand under the side of the crying baby's head to hold it up and the other hand under his hard belly. Then with Lucas' help, she stood up and gently began to swing the baby from side to side. In just a little while, the boy burped a hardy burp and calmed. His little eyes focused on a rock on the ground and soon the movement began to lull him to sleep. "The king did not die peacefully."

Jessup took a deep breath, determined to hold back her tears. "They killed him, Somehow I knew they would. Did John of Surrey take the throne?"

"I do not know. Neil wants to speak with you when you allow it. Perhaps he knows more."

"Please go get him, I will hear it all."

Glenna turned the baby toward Lucas to show him again how she had her hands. Then she put the boy face down on his mother's stomach so Lucas could then pick him up. "I will bring Neil straight away."

CHAPTER III

"What do you suggest we do?" Greer asked. She let go of her sister's arm, bent down and picked a wild flower.

"I do not know. Perhaps Neil can tell the lads to let me be."

"Neil is a powerful lad, but I doubt he holds that much authority. He might tell them, but they will still want to be near you. They would only be less bold about it."

Clare brushed loose strands of hair away from her face and frowned. "You mean they will become sleight of hand like the clerics. I could not endure that."

"In that case, I find no other answer save telling them yourself."

"Each separately or might I make a declaration?"

"There is hardly an occasion to make a declaration, at least not that I have seen. However, once you begin a rumor there is no stopping it in this place. When it comes to gossip, the Highlanders are far worse than the English."

"What could this rumor say exactly?" asked Clare.

"That, my beloved sister, we must carefully decide."

"We could say I am not inclined to fall in love."

"Aye, but it is not enough. We must give them a valid reason or they will ignore it."

Nearly at the corral, she glanced up and noticed three men standing just inside the fence watching her. One of them was Ben and when she looked his wife, Alison, who was not far away training one of the new colts, was glaring at her husband. Ben saw the look on his wife's face, quickly turned away and went back to work. Just as quickly, Clare turned around and started back to the cottage. "I will tell them my heart yet belongs to a man who died recently."

Hurrying to catch up, Greer giggled. "Well are you not the clever one. I would never have thought of such a convincing lie."

Clare wanted to scream -- it is not a lie! Instead, she looked away so her sister could not see the anguish in her eyes. She should tell Greer, she knew, but she was not yet able to accept Alcott's death, let alone talk about it. No, she wanted to wait, to find a place where she could be alone, to let it seep into her consciousness and to cry where no one would see her.

*

Jessup's baby was sound asleep in his box, in the shade of a tree outside, when Glenna brought Neil back to her cottage. Lucas set out a third chair and they all sat down not far from Jessup's bed to comfort her.

"…they believe it was he who sent the lads to slay the king," Neil finished explaining.

Everyone expected her to collapse in tears, but Jessup was livid. "George of Leics? The throne of England is now sat upon by a callous, foul tempered, braggart of a lad who never misses an opportunity to lure some unsuspecting lass into his bed. I should have killed the lad when I had the chance."

Neil could not help smiling at her colorful description. "No doubt half of England wishes you had."

"Unfortunately, I was content to make him promise not to pursue me further. The unforgivable, loathsome, black hearted scoundrel! Half of England may wish I had killed him, but the other half has their hands in his purse. It is *that* half Scotland must keep in careful regulation. My beloved Henry must be turning over in his grave."

"Jessup, I must know -- exactly how dangerous is George of Leics to Scotland?"

Jessup closed her eyes and tried to find the right words. "Scotland should do all she can to stay clear of this lad. He is quick to anger and needs little to incite him. He is also arrogant, brutal and said to enjoy killing. I doubt he cares one whit about Scotland except to possess her." Finally, tears began to cloud Jessup's eyes. "I should not have left Henry, I was his only friend."

*

Wickerly Castle, complete with three floors and five towers of varying heights, sat high on a hill at the end of a winding road. The bottom floor offered no windows at all, only a heavy wooden door which was rendered impenetrable, by virtue of three well-spaced iron slats with heavy iron latches.

At one end of the great hall on the first floor, stood a canopy that denoted the rank of the inhabitants, and also shielded them from the cold drafts coming from the upper floors. It was under this canopy Alcott of Cumberland sat with his mother, his three sisters and his squire, to watch the passing parade of mourners come to bid farewell to his father, the Lord of Wickerly.

News of his father's death came to Alcott late in the night as he slept on a wooden box frame bed, with a grid of ropes that held up a feather stuffed mattress, a pillow and the mountain of blankets necessary to keep him warm.

His large upstairs bedchamber had three tall, narrow windows too small for an uninvited man to gain entrance, and although wooden shutters closed off some of the cold air, they were grossly inefficient. The lack of natural light necessitated a multitude of iron, tricot candle holders situated both on his various trunks and affixed along the walls.

And when his steward came to light the candles and interrupt his sleep, news of the death was a solemn yet joyous occasion. It meant the suffering was ended for his father. Alcott could at last collect his beloved Clare and make her his wife. How ironic that losing a father he loved meant he could finally have the woman he loved.

The interment seemed to take forever with three days of mourning, the cleric's elongated service and the long procession from the great hall to the family burial plot. After that, it would have been unseemly to rush away when his new title and responsibilities demanded so much of his attention. His grieving mother and sisters also needed his comfort and he was left with no option, but to send his steward to the market with a letter for Clare explaining the news and the delay.

It was at the market on an otherwise tiresome day that he first saw the beautiful Clare. An ordinary market, it was filled with all manner of tables holding spices, woolens, foot wear, wooden platters of fresh fruits, various vegetables and flasks of wine. Gown makers showed off their needle crafts and iron workers showed off the latest latches and candle holders. Men of all shapes and sizes shouted tempting offers and a pig, let loose by a careless boy, nearly ran Alcott down.

Clare wore dowdy clothing and a hood that half shielded her face, yet when she briefly glanced at him, she had the most pleasing blue eyes he had ever seen. Alcott set out at once to make her acquaintance. The woman with her was Marlow, who often came to the market on behalf of the Abbey to barter for items not manufactured by them, such as rope, plates and goblets. On an earlier occasion, Alcott accidentally bumped into Marlow, which enabled him to gain her acquaintance, slight though it was.

On the day he first saw Clare, Alcott quickly became interested in the goblets too and when Marlow finally noticed him, he bowed to her curtsey and held his breath. It took a moment, but she at last remembered her manners and introduced him to the magnificent Clare. The moment their eyes locked, he felt an attachment like none other. It was not just her beauty, but her soul seemed to be reaching out to him.

Daily he returned to the market hoping to see her again, but she never returned. A week or two later, he sought a closer acquaintance with Marlow and pummeled her with questions. At last, Marlow relented -- Clare was not practicing to become a nun.

Alcott's heart leapt for joy.

He rode straight away to the Abbey and asked to see her, but he was denied. The reasoning of the rector seemed far insufficient, but what could he do? Alcott was not yet a man of influence and power. Not only that, he realized he could not take Clare to wife without losing his inheritance.

If only he could forget her...but he could not. The likelihood of making Clare his bride seemed out of the question until one day he hit upon an idea -- he would write and bribe Marlow to take the missive to her.

Another week passed without an answer and all manner of suspicions crossed his mind -- was she rejecting him out of hand, did she not get the letter, could she even read and write?

Then on the eighth day her answer came. Not only could she read and write, her hand was excellent, her words intelligent and her encouragement, slight though it might be, was indeed there. He could hardly contain his elation and set out straight away to write again. For weeks they exchanged letters, each telling of their hopes and dreams until their glorious obsession suddenly came to a halt -- Clare feared the rectors had found his letters and begged him to stop sending so many for fear of dreaded punishment on her part.

*

"Gone? What do you mean she is gone?" Alcott had a thousand things to clear up so he could claim his bride, but his steward's words echoing in the great hall captured all his attention.

"Lord Wickerly, do sit down. I fear the news has drained the color from your face." Stuart of Cumberland tried to look stately in his blue tunic with the white trim and Alcott's father's crest, but he was not an ample man and no matter what he did, the clothing hung loosely from his shoulders.

"Answer me! What happened?"

Stuart grimaced. "I took the missive to Miss Marlow as you requested and she gave the bad news. She said another letter came not three weeks past telling Clare you were dead."

"What? Who told this lie?"

"You need not shout, I am getting to that." Stuart was not always bold, but since the death of the elder Lord Wickerly, Alcott's demeanor changed to something more threatening right before his eyes. Stuart soon determined that he best not let the man get the better of him. A battle of wits once lost was lost forever.

"Speak up man!"

Stuart puffed his cheeks, rubbed the back of his neck and stalled just a little bit longer. "Marlow now believes one of the priests sent the message. The man delivering it claimed he was your steward, my lord, but of course I am your only steward."

Standing near a wall, Alcott slumped against it and bowed his head, "Where has she gone?"

"Her sister came to rescue her."

Alcott perked right up. "Greer? Clare thought her sister lost to her. But that is good news. Greer will see she is well taken care of."

"'Tis not good news. With her sister came four Highlanders. They offered the price and took her away with a multitude of other women."

"A multitude?"

"Aye, some thirty or forty, Marlow was uncertain of the exact number. But my lord, the news gets more dreadful still. The Highlands have suffer a severe shortage of women since the plague and they came looking for willing brides."

"Brides?" Alcott slumped back against the wall and closed his eye. "That is *not* good news. This multitude of women were willing to become brides to Highlanders they had not even seen?"

"It was that or become nuns against their will. I myself cannot decide which would be worse for a woman. We hear such dreadful things about these Highlanders. I once heard of a…"

"At least we know they have gone north. Someone must have seen them. One cannot move so many women without anyone's notice. Send men to inquire and report back. Tell them there will be a great reward for the one who brings me news of a true sighting."

Stuart was stunned, "My lord, certainly you do not mean to go into the Highlands to find her. 'Tis unthinkable."

"Living life without her is unthinkable. Do as I say, Stuart, send the soldiers and then begin preparations. I will leave you in charge here, unless you wish to go to Scotland with me."

"With your exalted permission, I will remain here."

Alcott thought about it for a moment and then smiled. "You are Scot by half and you speak Gaelic. I have changed my mind, I need you to go with me."

"My lord, I protest. It is too dangerous for one as feeble as I."

"In that case, I leave it up to you to find two of my best fighters to go with us."

"Four English men going into the Highlands alone? We will die on the first day."

"Not if I say I carry a message for the king of Scotland."

Stuart pondered the idea. "It might do. What message?"

"That, my good man, will be my charge. I will go to our new king, tell him I intend to go into Scotland and ask if he has a message to give the Scottish king. He will have, naturally. Never have I known George of Leics not to have a message -- no matter who the recipient."

CHAPTER IV

Clare continued to walk with her sister up the glen toward the cottages. The pain in her broken heart was so great, she dared not even look at her sister for fear it would show. It was the first time in a fortnight she allowed herself to think of Alcott and now she actually said out loud that he was dead. With those words she managed to shatter her self-imposed illusion that somehow it was all a mistake.

All she had of him was his last letter. The other missives disappeared and she was desperately searching for them when Marlow brought the news of Alcott's death. Thankfully, his last letter was in the pocket of her brown robe when she was rescued and she still had it. Now, she kept it under the leather belt that held up her pleated MacGreagor plaid. It was all she had left of him -- all she would ever have of him, and her heart ached so deeply she wanted to die with him.

Clare glanced at her sister's concerned look and pushed the painful and unwelcome thoughts of Alcott to the back of her mind. "I would like to go riding, if it is allowed."

"It is allowed, although Neil does not let us go without lads to protect us. It is not safe."

"Would Brendan take us?"

"I will ask him, but sister you just rode most of the way here from England. Was it not enough?"

"Not nearly. I have not been on a horse in years and I did so love it when I was learning to ride."

"I see. Very well then, we must have two lads to take us but Brendan will choose the other lad for us."

"I would also like to learn weaving, would that be allowed?"

"Sweet child, you may do nearly anything you wish." Greer paused to think for a moment. "Our best weaver is Kadick. Would you object to her showing you?"

"Of course not. I hoped to become her friend on the journey here, but she was never without Donnahail. He truly loves her, does he not?"

"I have never seen anything like the two of them. It is as though they were always meant to be together. That settles it then, we will visit Kadick and ask if she is willing to teach you."

Clare was pleased. What she needed was something to do so she could forget the constant, unbearable agony in her heart. Alcott was dead and there was nothing she could do or say to bring him back. Time heals all wounds, or so the nuns said when she was little and missed her mother. Then later her hurt turned to bitterness and the nuns taught her forgiveness, which was a much more difficult lesson to learn. Time would indeed erase the memory of Alcott, if she could manage to outlive the suffering.

"Speaking of Brendan …" Greer said, spotting her future husband walking toward them. She waited for him to arrive, gave him a quick hug and then let him take her hand. "Clare would like to go riding, will you take us?"

"I will be honored, but Greer I bring bad news. The king of England was not ill, he was done in."

*

Kadick was more than willing to teach Clare and even asked Slade to build another loom. She went to the cottage for two days and carefully watched Kadick's every move until she thought she had it memorized. But when she tried it on her own, it was a lot harder than it looked.

Kadick was a good sport about it, although it meant putting her work behind, and with so many new women to clothe, the work appeared to be never ending. By the end of the second day, they decided Clare should begin the next day with smaller plaids for the children and then move up to the more difficult work. Kadick was pleasant but Clare was not convinced she had the talent necessary for weaving. If not that, what?

As she left Kadick's cottage, Clare had to admit she was not concentrating well and it was time. She needed to go off by herself and mourn the loss of the man she loved. It was indeed time to let go and to let herself feel something. She was no good to anyone with it all held inside so tightly.

She did not mean to wander so far away, but once she began to walk through the forest, she kept right on going until she heard a disturbing clicking noise. She stopped, turned to face the direction she believed the noise was coming from, and tried to find its origin.

With a finger held to his lips to caution her to be quiet a man slowly stood up.

She was not afraid of him, after all he wore a MacGreagor kilt, but when he pointed and she looked, two Haldane warriors were walking through the trees only a few yards away. They had not spotted her, so when the MacGreagor motioned for her to get down, she quickly obeyed.

Then she watched the MacGreagor return to his hiding place behind a tall bush and waited. The wait seemed endless, but after a time, the MacGreagor stood back up and came to her.

"It is safe, you can stand up now." he said, offering his hand.

"You speak English?"

"If you can understand me, then I suppose I do."

"Have you been watching me?"

Tristan raised an eyebrow. He possibly just saved her life and instead of being grateful, she was accusing him of something. "Nay, *they* have been watching you. *I* have been watching them. I suggest you go back with the others straight away, if not sooner."

"I intend to." She was quite annoyed. First, he unnerved her with that clicking noise, interrupted her solitude and now he had mocked her…twice.

"Good."

"Good what?"

"It is good that you intend to go home."

She started to walk away, paused and turned back. "Which way?"

Tristan pointed west and then watched her turn and begin to walk back through the thick foliage. When her skirt caught on a bush, he rolled his eyes. "I suppose you need my help."

"I can manage." Clare yanked and yanked on the cloth but it would not come free. "Tell me, have you learned any other English words save 'suppose?'"

He was not impressed with her tone of voice, covered the distance to her in short order, unhooked her skirt and put both hands on his hips. "I suppose not."

She had no idea why this man irritated her so, but she was happy to be hurrying away. Moments before he interfered, she was about to cry and let her heart believe Alcott was dead. But now he ruined it.

Of course, it was not true he interrupted her solitude; the Haldanes were actually to blame for that. Suddenly, Clare was ashamed of herself and made a mental note to apologize the next time she saw him, whoever he was.

She abruptly stopped and turned around. Clare expected to see the MacGreagor right behind her, but he was not there and even after searching the woods with her eyes, she could not see him. "How long do you suppose the Haldanes have been watching me?"

"I thought you did not like the word suppose."

He made her smile.

"Go home little lass. It is not safe here."

Still he had not given up his hiding place and she did not know in which direction she should nod, so she just turned around and started walking again. "Forgive me for not thanking you earlier."

There it was finally -- a show of appreciation. The English woman might not be so ill mannered after all. She was as beautiful as he had heard, but Tristan paid little attention to the other men's gossip, because he was not certain he should have a wife. He learned scouting from his father, loved calling the forest his real home and could not always abide the confines of a cottage which, if he was not mistaken, wives were quite fond of.

More importantly, the clan's scout was on the first line of defense and was often killed by an enemy even before a war began. His father died at the age of twenty-seven and his mother lived another fifteen years, mourning the loss of her husband every day. Why then, would a good man do that to the woman he loved? Yet his parents loved each other very much and his mother always claimed the years she had with her husband were worth the pain of losing him.

Tristan stood up and continued to follow Clare through the forest, ready to crouch down should she stop again. Women were always unpredictable and usually unreasonable. His thoughts sparked a memory and brought a smile to his lips. When he complained that his mother was being unreasonable, his father confided, "You think lasses are unreasonable, and I think it -- but lasses do not believe it."

He quietly slipped from tree to tree, watching Clare and protecting her in case the Haldanes came back. But before she reached the edge of the forest, Clare stopped again. He meant to remain quiet and let her be, but she took a very deep breath and then wiped a tear off her cheek. "I am here," he found himself saying.

She did not turn to look at him. "I know, I heard you."

"You heard me?" He left his hiding place and walked to her. "This is very serious. I have spent years practicing to be quiet and now I am caught by a woman whom I was not even trying to sneak up on."

She turned and tried to smile, "Unfortunately for you, I was raised in the Abbey where silence was required on most occasions. It sharpens ones hearing, you see. At times silence is so tedious, the sound of a mouse skittering across a floor is the height of excitement."

His was a crooked smile, not at all unpleasant and Clare noticed.

His hair was not dark like Alcott's and his eyes were blue instead of brown, but his hair was clean and his eyes were brightened by his smile. At length Clare turned away. "I did not mean to stare. I have not been this close to a man in…Well there were always the clerics, but you are pleasing to look at and the clerics were not."

He was flattered and surprised by her openness. "I am happy to please you. Why were you crying?"

"I am fine now, thank you. I must get back before Greer begins to fret." With that, she walked into the glen and headed home.

Tristan did not take his eyes off her until one of the other men came to protect and walk her home. But before she accepted the other man's assistance, she looked back and something in his heart began to stir.

CHAPTER V

With their king newly dead, it was a time of mourning for all the English brides, and the Highlander men were more than willing to make themselves available in case any of them needed comfort. That is, until Clare walked by. Her presence caused the men to lose their concentration, and the expressions on the faces of the women turned from sorrow to irritation.

Clare could have cared less and paid them no attention. When she got back to the cottage, she was pleased to find Brendan and Greer sitting outside on a tree stump. "I hope you have not been waiting for me."

"Have you learned to cook yet?" Greer teased.

Clare played along. "I will see what I can do, but it might take a few days. Are you hungry?"

"Never mind. You are in luck, I baked bread this morning just for you." Greer lightly hugged Clare. "Sister, have I your permission to explain to Brendan why you do not wish to marry just now?"

There was a hint of hurt in Clare's eyes when she nodded and went inside, Greer thought. My sister has learned to lie very well indeed, yet there was something … Too soon, Greer dismissed the thought and went back into Brendan's arms.

"What is her reason?" he asked.

"Clare's heart belongs to a lad who died recently."

"I see. Does she cry often? Because I know at least ten lads who would…"

Greer glared at her intended. "You will soon be her brother, do not forget. Brothers protect, not conspire against, their sisters."

Brendan playfully swelled his chest. "I am honored to protect my dear sister, but surely you will not object if I accept a bribe or two when she is ready to seek a husband."

Greer rolled her eyes.

*

Clare's ability to distract the men and the death of the king might have postponed the taking of husbands for a time, but it did not stop the rumors and there were plenty to be had. Both Walrick and Gelson returned with the same news - the English people hated the new king and they were trying to find a woman named, Charlet. Charlet was not a common name and Neil was more than a little worried.

Few knew Charlet's real story and most in the MacGreagor Clan were too young to remember who she was or what happened. But Neil remembered exactly what his father told him and took a vow to keep Charlet's whereabouts a secret.

"It is a French name," Glenna said. She sat in a chair in their bedchamber brushing her long lovely hair before bed, even though sleep would tangle it again.

Neil got into bed and waited for her to join him. "I do not know where she got the name. Perhaps the old king suggested it. Father said he was a good king who loved his niece very much. He went to great lengths to save Charlet's life."

"What age do you think she is now, providing she survived the plague?"

"Well, she was just a couple of years younger than my Aunt Rachel who was a good ten years older than me."

"Then she is still young enough to take the crown...if she yet lives."

"As I recall, my love, it was you who were charged with finding out what happened to her."

Glenna finally laid the brush down on the table and went to peek in the box at their sleeping daughter. Satisfied, she walked to the other side of the bed. "True, but no one seems to know what's become of her. Why do these rumors bother you so?"

He watched her lift the covers and climb into bed next to him. Then he opened his arms and drew her to him. "I worry it is some sort of trap. Suppose the new king only wants to entice her back so he can dispose of her."

"What do these rumors say, exactly?"

"They say there is rebellion in the wind against the new king and they want to restore the throne to her."

"Or her children?"

"I had not thought of that. Charlet took a new name hoping to avoid this very thing."

Glenna snuggled against him and closed her tired eyes. "Are you thinking of trying to find her?"

"She is a MacGreagor. Who better to protect her than the rest of the MacGreagors?"

"Perhaps Charlet went to live with another clan once the new laird took over the Cameron Clan."

"Perhaps so. At any rate, the English are looking for Charlet and must not know she changed her name. I have hardly thought of her in years. She was in my father's care and she…" When Neil looked, Glenna was fast asleep.

*

Alcott returned from seeing the king as quickly as he could and upon entering the great hall of his castle, he demanded to hear Stuart's report.

"A large band of highlanders, together with many women passed through the land of the Swinton's. They claim the MacGreagors have her," Stuart said.

"MacGreagors? I have heard of this clan. Did the Swintons say where they were headed?"

"North, they rode due north. My lord, must I go with you? Give over the land you promised at your father's death and be done with me."

"Done with you? How can I be done with a man who knows all my secrets? The land will surely be yours, but I will never be done with you or you with me."

After many years as steward to Alcott of Cumberland, Stuart suspected the best approach with this man was no approach at all -- until an opportunity presented itself to take the upper hand. Perhaps going with him into Scotland was not such a bad idea after all. Perhaps he would go with him and come back without him. "As you wish, my lord."

"Is everything ready?"

"Nearly everything. When do we leave?"

"At first light tomorrow."

"Then you have a message from the King of England to give to the King of Scotland?"

"I do," Alcott answered.

"I am pleased to hear it. Finally, your friendship with that wretched excuse for a man has provided some benefit."

Alcott walked to the table near the canopy in the great hall and poured himself some of the sweeter wine the English preferred. "That wretched excuse for a man, you call him, is giving me the most beautiful woman in all of England."

Stuart accepted the chalice of wine from his superior and downed half. "I pray you did not mention her beauty to him. You know how he desires pretty women and if you are not careful, George will take her from you and spoil her … if the Highlanders have not already done it."

It was the very thing that had plagued Alcott's mind for days. If the Highlanders had already forced her, he might as well leave Clare with them and his trip would be for nothing. He loved her, he truly did, but her chastity was the only guarantee his bloodline would not become tainted…and that was far more important than love. For just a brief moment, Alcott considered how unpleasant being forced might have been for Clare. But women were forced all the time and it was not a death sentence.

"Second thoughts, my lord?"

"Not at all Stuart. When you see her, you will understand. The exquisite Clare will be my wife and I will be the envy of all men, even the king himself."

*

She never said a word when Tristan lifted her onto the horse and stayed by her side while Clare swung her leg over and got comfortable. Then she watched him mount his horse and together they waited for Greer and Brendan to bring their mares up beside them. Lost in their own little world, Greer and Brendan hardly paid any attention to where they were or who they were with. They were so in love, they might have ridden their horses off the edge of the world and never noticed

"What would you like to see?" Tristan asked Clare.

She did not really care, but because he asked, she looked around and then pointed to the highest hill. "May we go up there?" He didn't even bother to nod, she noticed, but when he led the way, she followed. It felt good to be away from all the men who stared and all the women who glared. She tried not to concern herself with any of them, but each day became harder and harder. Even so, what was outside was nothing compared to the turmoil inside her.

It was as though she lived in a circle of confusion where complete thoughts and sentences were neither welcome nor expected. Every once in a while, his name -- Alcott -- would invade, but somehow it did not cause her to pause in her original thought. She was, she believed, quite mad.

"Clare?"

Tristan said her name three more times before it registered he was talking to her. They were at the crest of the hill and she could not recall how she got there. "Ah … it is very beautiful."

"I asked if you are cold."

"Oh, I see."

As soon as he heard about her loss, he felt bad for being so off-handed with her in the forest. And just now, her eyes were easily betraying the unbearable torture going on inside her heart and mind. She reminded him of a lost child, one he wanted to sweep up into his arms and save from all harm. "It is Tristan."

"What?" Clare asked.

"You asked my name."

"Did I?"

Greer and Brendan were taking their time climbing up the hillside and when he looked, Tristan noticed other men standing below watching him. That meant holding Clare even just to comfort her, was completely out of the question. He intentionally moved his horse a little farther away. "Clare, have you ever seen a waterfall?"

The mention of a waterfall seemed to bring her out of her mindless fog. "I have read of such things. Do you have one?"

Tristan smiled, "I do not have it. I mean, it is not mine, but I know where one is. Would you like to see it?"

"I would like that very much."

"You said you read about them? You know how to read?"

"The priests were training me to become a scribe before..."

"Before what?"

She finally looked at him. She might as well look at him, she didn't seem to be able to actually take in the beauty of the view. "Before I refused to do something. After that, I was relegated to the gardens."

"I understand." He truly did understand. His occasional venture into England afforded him the opportunity to sometimes hear scandals about pregnant, unmarried nuns. "Do you want to talk about him?"

Clare wrinkled her brow, "Who?"

"The lad who died."

She quickly turned away. "I cannot."

"Then you shall not." Tristan let it go that easily and changed the subject. "We will look at the scenery instead. I never get tired of looking at our beautiful green glen." Greer and Brendan, he noticed, were stopped and intensely discussing something. Then Clare began to talk about Alcott and got his full attention.

"I only saw him up close once. The clerics would not let him come to see me, so we exchanged forbidden letters. Once he came to deliver a message from his father and I saw him from afar then, but..."

"But you loved him?"

"I loved him. They said he died of an injury that would not heal. The thought of his suffering is most difficult to bear and I wonder sometimes, if my name was the last on his lips."

Tristan watched a single tear roll down her cheek. "Why did he not come and take you from the Abbey? Surely you were not a prisoner there."

"Until I met him, I felt like a prisoner by virtue of not having anywhere else to go. Greer promised to come back for me someday, but I had given up on that. Alcott intended to come for me; it just was not yet time."

CHAPTER VI

That was a concept Tristan was having difficulty understanding. In his world a man loves a woman and makes her his wife. What time could possibly be the wrong time? He wanted to ask her more questions, but Greer and Brendan finally managed to join them and all conversation about Alcott abruptly stopped.

It wasn't until he led them down the hill, took the path beside the river, and found the waterfall, that the opportunity once more presented itself.

Clare stood on a large rock near the water's edge with her arms folded. The air smelled sweet, the sky was a bright blue and Tristan stood right behind her in case she started to fall.

It was not an enormous waterfall, only about eight feet tall, but the crystal clear water cascading into the blue pond took her breath away. "It is magnificent."

"I do not believe many others have found this place." Tristan watched Brendan lead Greer on around the large pond until they found a rock to sit on. Then Tristan looked back to make sure the horses were content to drink and nibble on the long grass.

"I love the sound of the water. It is soothing, somehow," Clare said.

"It is indeed."

"Tristan, I want to thank you."

He marveled when she said his name. It sounded almost musical and it was as though he had never heard it spoken before. "Thank me for what?"

"For letting me talk about Alcott. I did not think I could or ever would be able to, but you listened and I am comforted."

"In that case, perhaps you will allow me one question?"

"What?"

"What could have been more important to him than taking you to wife?"

She glanced back at Tristan and smiled slightly "I was not so pleased with that myself. However, his explanation had merit and I could not blame him for it. His father would not have approved of the marriage and without an inheritance, he had no way to provide for me."

Tristan was not impressed. A man who truly loves a woman finds a way. "I suppose we are different from the English in that regard. A clan works together to provide for the lass and children, and no lad must await an inheritance to provide for them."

Clare turned completely around to face him, "Why Tristan MacGreagor, you do not approve. I can hear it in your voice."

"I did not mean…"

"Of course you meant it." She lowered her head and lightly bit her lip, "If you promise not to tell, I will share a secret with you. I did not approve either."

"But he was your only hope of escaping the monastery."

"Precisely." She turned back around and listened to the sound of the falling water for a while longer. "It was not as though I were in any danger or would not be fed if he left me where I was. It only meant we could not be together until after his father died."

Tristan was not sure he wanted to hear any more of this. Having lost his own beloved father, he could not understand a man wishing his father would die so he could take the wife he wanted. It riled Tristan to the bone and he did not trust himself to speak. Fortunately for Alcott, he was already dead.

"There is another thing that bothered me, however," Clare said at length.

"Which was?"

"Alcott said he lived in Wickerly Castle and was a wealthy man. If that were so, I wonder why did he not board me in a place where we could be together occasionally. But I suppose his father would have found out."

"Aye, the English are quite the gossips."

Clare rolled her eyes. It was MacGreagor gossips who told Tristan about her Alcott's death, and the word spread much more quickly than she expected.

"Have you thought there might be another reason he did not rescue you?"

"Such as?"

"You are quite becoming. A lad might want you kept out of sight so no other lad could tempt you away." She didn't say a word and when she didn't he wondered if she had already guessed that was Alcott's purpose.

"I do not want to believe that of him. How very cruel to have left me in a place he knew I sorely hated, simply to keep me all to himself."

Tristan could hardly blame the man for thinking that way. The more he spent time with Clare, the more he learned to appreciate her. "Perhaps he did not realize you were suffering."

"I said as much in my letters, so I doubt he could have misunderstood. Oh well, it is of no importance now."

"I suppose not."

She smiled and turned around to face him again, "There is that word again -- suppose. Promise you will never change. I am fond of people who do not positively know the answer to every question. It is a welcome change." Tristan had not meant to, she realized, but he had given her a great deal to think about.

He offered his hand to help her climb down off the rock. "Your sister and Brendan have been discussing something serious, or so it seems."

"I noticed that too. Shall we find out what it is or do you advise we stay clear of it?"

Tristan was honored she would ask him. "I fear it has to do with a disagreement. I say we wait."

They did not have to wait long. Once Greer noticed them watching her, she motioned for Tristan and her sister to join them. Soon, all four were seated on the rocks farther away from the waterfall where it was a bit more quiet.

"Sister, you do not look pleased. What is it?" asked Clare.

Greer took her hand. "I have been approached by some of the other lasses."

"About what?"

"About you."

Clare drew in a breath. "Go on."

"They believe the lads will not choose a wife until you are either married or..."

"Or gone?" When her sister nodded, Clare could not help but slump. "They do not believe I am in mourning?"

"They have not seen you cry. It is a bit unnatural, you are aware. It was a lie anyway, so it is of little matter."

Tristan started to say something but before he could, Clare lightly touched his hand. "I am a little cold. May I borrow your extra plaid?" He nodded, went to his horse and got it for her.

"When must I leave?" Clare asked as soon a Tristan wrapped the cloth around her shoulders and sat back down.

Greer burst into tears. "I am going with you."

"The hell you are!" Brendan got up and began to pace beside the pond.

Greer managed to pull herself together long enough to blurt out, "Brendan, I left her once and I will not forsake her again."

Brendan quickly disagreed. "The lasses have no say in who stays and who goes. Only Neil can banish someone and he would not do it without just cause. Jealous lasses are not just cause!"

"Do calm yourself, Brendan," Clare said. "I do not want to stay where I am not wanted, just cause or not. I can live in England as easily as I can live here."

Greer shook her head. "How? Are you to become servant to some idle lord and lady, who cannot so much as wash their own hair? I will not hear of it."

"Perhaps I could take a position in an orphanage."

The more Brendan thought of losing Greer the more enraged he became. "Perhaps you could stay here too! If it is children you are wanting to take care of, we are about to have a glut of them with all these new brides."

Clare covered her face with her hands. "How am I to walk among them now? It was hard enough before I knew they wanted me gone."

Tristan had not said a word, but about this, he could no longer be quiet. "I am fascinated by this event. Not long ago the whole clan was chastised for looking down on Kadick's mark, and so soon they have done it again -- only this time because of beauty. It seems we never learn."

Still greatly annoyed, Brendan glared at his longtime friend. "I am happy you are fascinated, but it hardly solves the problem."

Tristan smiled anyway. "It might when Neil gets wind of this. At times, I think he regrets bringing so many English to us all at once. Now he will be sure he made a mistake."

Despite her tears, Greer started to laugh. "He had no choice. The wagons at the Abbey were full of lasses and one mention of husbands was all the temptation they needed."

On the way back, Tristan waited until the still arguing Greer and Brendan had fallen behind and were paying little attention. "Why did you not tell your sister about Alcott?"

Clare shrugged. "I got word of his death just the day before she came for me and she was so happy, I did not want to spoil it for her."

"Why not tell her now?"

"I have been asking myself the same question. I wanted the lads to stay away and when I gave that excuse, Greer just assumed it was a lie. Tristan, I do not even remember half the journey here. In fact, I do not remember climbing that hill with you this morning. My mind is addled half the time and the other half, I cannot bring myself to speak his name. Have I gone daft, do you think?"

"You are not daft, just diverted. When my father died, it was the same for me. This evening I will come and take you for a walk. If the lasses think you prefer me, perhaps they will drop their demand for you to leave."

"And the lads will stay away also?"

"That, I cannot promise." He smiled and she smiled in return.

CHAPTER VII

Tristan took her riding as a favor to Brendan and although he did not regret taking the time, he had not intended to see Clare again. Then she needed him and it was natural to offer to help. He would do the same for any woman, he reminded himself. He took his soap, his clean clothing, walked out the door of his cottage and headed to the loch to bathe.

The water was warmer than usual and Tristan could not help but linger -- and think about Clare. She was a sensible woman, but very vulnerable by virtue of her sheltered upbringing. A man need only set wealth and a castle in front of a woman like Clare and she would follow him anywhere...and perhaps do anything to hold his favor. Fortunately, Alcott died before he could harm her further, and it was a good thing too, because the thought of what might have happened was starting to get under Tristan's skin.

*

They did not walk alone that evening. Not only did Greer and Brendan walk with them but also Donnahail and Kadick. Somehow a rumor began that the women wanted Clare gone, and some felt the need to show their allegiance to Clare. Then Gill and a very pregnant Ralin joined. Walrick was busy so Steppen and Jonrose came without husbands and by the time Neil and Glenna looked out the third story window of the Keep, there were thirty people walking with Clare down the glen.

Neil put his arm around Glenna's shoulders. "Is there something I should know about?"

"Nay...unless you have a desire to get between squabbling lasses."

Neil's eyes shot wide open and he pretended great fear, "Please, any punishment but squabbling lasses."

"That is what I thought." Glenna leaned her head against his shoulder. "Let us see if they can work this one out on their own."

*

All the way from England, Alcott tried to remember why the name MacGreagor sounded so familiar. He could remember his father having no dealings with them, nor a war in which they were defeated. But the name...where had he heard the name? Finally, he remembered. It was with the MacGreagors the old king hid his niece, Charlet. He guessed he was only one of a few people who knew that and he told no one. He might need that information to save his life someday, if he ever fell out of favor with the king.

Alcott's plot to make the Highlanders think he carried a message for the king of Scotland worked. The clans they encountered dared not stop him and fortunately he was going in the right direction to make it believable. The King of Scotland, or so everyone believed, was as far north as a Scot could get.

The Clan Swinton warned of a marked woman, the MacPhearsons were not happy to see them and the Englishmen were certain they would not survive crossing Haldane property. The Haldane, though they did not approach the English, watched them from the top of every hill until they were off Haldane land.

At last, Alcott and his men turned into the glen of the MacGreagors. They wore red English tunics, black stockings and a terrified Stuart held up a flag exhibiting the Crest of the Lord of Wickerly. Almost immediately, a man in the forest somewhere nearby let loose a shrill whistle. Soon other whistles could be heard farther away until the last one sounded at a village they could barely see in the distance.

"How clever of them," Alcott breathed. "They can see us but we cannot see them."

In the great hall, Neil, Walrick and Gelson raced up the two flights of stairs and then to the bedchamber window that faced south.

"They are very brave to come into Scotland with only four lads," said Gelson.

Walrick ran his fingers through his hair. "Very brave or very stupid." The three of them watched for a while longer before he spoke again. "Shall I welcome them or kill them?"

Neil grinned. "Are you not curious? I will hear what drives a lad to do something this ill-advised."

Gelson chuckled. "The only thing I know of is a…"

"*A lass*," all three said at the same time."

Neil laughed and slapped Walrick on the back. "Which one? I say it is Carol, the milk maid."

"Nay," Gelson argued, "there is another who has a faraway look in her eye. What is her name? I…"

Neil started back down the stairs. "It is a good thing you already have a wife. You cannot even remember their names."

*

The room was deathly quiet when the four Englishmen entered the Scottish great hall to stand a respectable distance from Laird Neil MacGreagor. The MacGreagor was so big, he was an impressive figure and Alcott of Cumberland tried not to let himself be intimidated. Beside the giant was another man of equal size and a third who, thank goodness, was more of a normal size. But then, Alcott reminded himself that he was not there to fight. All three MacGreagors wore green kilts, white shirts and leather shoes that laced up to their knees.

Behind them stood three women, each looking at the English men as though they had never seen one before. One woman giggled and pointed at Alcott's short tunic, with a flounced skirt that ended just above his knees. Evidentially she thought his clothing were humorous and that made him glower at her. Unfortunately, he did not know he was glowering at Neil's wife.

Soon tired of the wordless face-off, Alcott turned to Stuart. "Tell them we have come for Clare."

Before Stuart could put the words into Gaelic, all three Highlanders looked incredulous. "Clare?" they all asked at once.

Neil rolled his eyes, Walrick laughed and Gelson was amazed. In Gaelic Gelson said, "Not Clare, she has been in a convent. How does a lad fall in love with a lass in a convent?"

"You have to pay the priest." Neil answered.

"Oh."

Of the four Englishmen, Stuart was the only one who understood Gaelic and he liked these men right off. They were good-natured and after spending days with no relief from Alcott's exalted stupidity, the MacGreagors were refreshing.

To get even with his superior for the promised land he was sure by now he would never get, Stuart did not repeat Alcott's words correctly. Instead, he said in Gaelic, "Do not let this lad leave with Clare." Stuart kept his face expressionless, but he saw in the MacGreagor's eyes a flicker of understanding.

It was quiet again and Alcott started to get unnerved. Why no answer? At least the highlanders recognized her name, they laughed when he brought it up. He leaned closer to Stuart, "Ask if they have her." He paused while Stuart asked, then waited for him to interpret the answer. "Aye, they have a woman named Clare."

"For pity sakes, Stuart, tell them I have come to fetch her."

Neil patiently listened to the man change the English into Gaelic. He was enjoying the spectacle, first of the arrogant lord completely out of his element in Scotland, and the poor interpreter who seemed to hate his employer. Finally, he said, "Nay."

"Nay what?" asked Alcott. He realized he was clenching his fists and made himself calm down. "Stuart, ask him to please explain what he means."

Stuart bowed his compliance and turned to Neil, "The idiot does not understand the word nay, apparently."

It was more than Neil could do to keep a straight face and as soon as some of the others began, he could not help but join in the laugher.

A stricken Stuart quickly turned to Alcott, "My lord, do forgive me. My Gaelic is...I must have gotten a word or two confused."

"I see." Alcott tightly closed his eyes and slowly opened them again. "Tell him I do not want to harm Clare, I want to marry her, if she will have me. She believes I am dead."

Neil only half heard what Stuart was saying. He did not like Alcott and he especially did not like the way he glared at Glenna, but he brought up a good point. Clare had the right to reject him herself. At last, he nodded for Luag to go get her.

*

Luag knew exactly which cottage was hers as did all the other unmarried men. And when he got there, he found Clare, Tristan, Greer and Brendan sitting outside talking. He was not happy to see Tristan, but he set that aside for now. "Clare, there is an Englishman here asking for you."

Clare quickly stood up. "Is it a cleric? I'll not go back to the Abbey, not ever!"

"Nay, he is not a priest."

Suddenly upset, Clare reached for Tristan's hand. "Who can it be? Will you come with me?"

He was surprised, but as soon as she collected her sister and Brendan for fortification too, he understood she had a foreboding and only wanted to feel safe.

A few moments later, they were standing in the great hall and Tristan was behind her holding a stunned Clare up from behind.

CHAPTER VIII

Clare's eyes were wide, her mouth agape and all she could do was stare at him. She did not run to him as a woman in love would have but at length, she did stand up a little straighter not needing Tristan's physical support quite so much. "They said you were dead."

Alcott went to her and took her limp hand. "I know, but as you can see, I am not dead. I have come to take you home finally."

Greer suddenly realized. "Do you mean you truly were in mourning? Oh sister, I am so sorry. I thought…"

But Clare ignored her and spoke to Alcott, "Your father has…"

"Passed," he answered. Alcott looked down to show the proper amount of respect for his departed father.

But when he raised his head he looked as though he was going to kiss her forehead. The thought of it made her stiffen. He looked so unimpressive compared to the Highlanders, and he was not nearly as handsome as she remembered. His hair was dark and so were his eyes, but this time his eyes were not soft. Instead, there was a hint of fury in them, a fury she did not want to see.

He wanted to get Clare away from these people in all possible haste, but Alcott had to know and was looking at Tristan when he asked, "Clare, has he spoiled you?"

"What?" She no longer leaned hard against him, but could still feel Tristan's muscles tighten. "You dare ask me that in front of others?"

"If you are to be my wife, I must know the truth. Besides, these are simple people who do not even speak our language."

"I see." Suddenly bold, Clare glanced at Neil and then turned around to look at her sister. "Alcott, how is your dearest friend?"

"You have not yet answered my question."

"True, but mine is far more interesting to these simple minded people who do not speak our language. Your dear friend is George of Leics, is he not?"

"George was quite well when last I saw him and I do not understand why you would bring up such a thing. Now answer my question? Has he spoiled you? I cannot have a wife who is not…"

"Chaste?" asked Neil in English.

A stunned Alcott quickly turned around.

But from behind Clare, Tristan tapped Alcott on the shoulder. "We could use a good lad like you to clean up after the horses. They tend to make a considerable mess and cleaning up their droppings quickly teaches a lad to mind his manners…even in the company of simple minded people."

Alcott began to back away from Clare, but Neil quickly came to him. "You are the bravest of lads entering Scotland with only four. I am quite enthralled. Come, share my wine and tell me all about your friend. He is the new king, is he not?"

Still shocked that Neil spoke English, he hesitantly nodded, let the giant take his arm and guide him to the table. Glenna took all the women, including Greer and Clare upstairs and soon the seats at the table were filled with Englishmen on one side and Scotsmen on the other, none of whom were certain what Laird MacGreagor was up to.

Tristan and Brendan stayed back, but were determined to wait for Greer and Clare.

Neil filled a goblet with wine and handed it to his guest. "We hear good things about this new king. Tell me, what do you like about him?"

Alcott cautiously looked at the Highlander faces across the table from him. "Like about him? Ah…well…he is fair minded on most occasions."

Neil was tempted to make the man struggle to find flattering things to say about his king a while longer for sport, but he wasn't sure he could abide the man's company for long. "How long have you known him?"

Alcott relaxed a little, on this subject he could speak easily. "We were raised in the same county, Cumberland naturally. We played together as…"

*

Seated across from him, Walrick finally caught Stuart's eye and asked, "None of them speak Gaelic?"

"Not a word. What would you like to know?"

"How do you intend to rid yourself of him?"

Stuart was shocked. "You know? But how…?"

"It is what I would do. The world is better off without lads like him."

"He promised to give over a nice section of property when his father died, but he has broken his promise. Now I am bound to him forever, unless I can do him in somehow."

Walrick drank some of his wine. "We will not do it for you unless he draws his sword, but we will not protect him either."

"Thank you." Stuart glanced at Alcott, who was still being grilled by Neil. "He only wants Clare to boast of her beauty to the king. They constantly try to out-do each other." Stuart was quiet for a moment. "You will not kill him unless he draws his sword?"

"Aye, unless he draws and aims to kill one of us."

"I am small yet in a fair fight, I might be able to do it myself. But the other two are loyal."

"I see. Then what you need is for us to provide you with a fair fight."

"Aye, and in return I will be a friend of the MacGreagors for life."

*

So far, Neil was not pleased with any of Alcott's answers. However he thought he had the man plied with enough wine to be forthright when he asked a more pertinent question. "Why is the king looking for Charlet?"

Alcott smiled, "I nearly forgot. I meant to ask you about her. Word has her being raised by the MacGreagors. Is it true?"

"Aye there was a lass named Charlet in our clan, but it was years ago. She is probably dead by now, if that was the one. Charlet is a fairly common name in the Highlands."

"Dead? Are you certain?"

"I am certain of nothing." The man's inability to hold his wine was becoming extremely irritating, so Neil decided to ask just one more time. "Why is the king of England looking for Charlet?"

"I do not know who is looking for her. They are talking about her all over England. Some say she is the rightful heir, but George will never relent. It is not in his blood to lose any sort of battle and especially not to a lass."

It was not the answer Neil wanted, but he believed it was the truth. He sent Brendan upstairs to get Clare and then waited, giving only short answers to all of Alcott's questions. As soon as she entered, all the men stood up. "Clare, do you wish to marry this lad?"

Alcott finally made it to his feet, "See here, MacGreagor, I..."

"Nay," Clare interrupted. "May I go now?"

"Aye." Neil smiled and watched her go, followed by Greer, Brendan and Tristan.

That was an end to it. Clare was a MacGreagor and it was time to send this English back to the hole he crawled out of. He noticed Alcott was not steady on his feet and nodded to Walrick. "See they are off our land and sent back to England."

Walrick helped Stuart take Alcott out the door and put him on his horse. He nodded as soon as Stuart mounted and then whispered instructions to the four men he was sending to escort them off the property.

*

She was calm all the way back and never said a word, but when they got to Greer's cottage, Clare could no longer maintain her composure. She was exhausted and did not hesitate to sit down on the tree stump near the cottage door and rest her face in her hands. "What a horrible little man and to think I put all my hopes and dreams in him."

Greer put a hand on her sister's shoulder, "Do you forgive me for not taking you seriously?"

"Only if you forgive me for not telling you."

"Only if you will tell me all about it later."

Clare couldn't help but giggle. "Everyone will soon know what a baboon I have been for ever loving a man like that."

Brendan wrinkled he brow. "What is a baboon?"

"It is a..."

But Tristan interrupted, "That is what I forgot to tell Neil. Clare can read and write."

Brendan was thrilled, "That is it! We have been looking for something the women cannot refute and we have found it. Someone who can read and write English is very useful to the clan."

"Then I will stay, but I do not yet want a husband. I want to learn freedom first, and learn to weave, and learn to laugh, and even to cry."

Greer wrinkled her brow. "Aye, but what are we going to tell all the lads? Telling them you do not want a husband will not likely keep them away for more than a day."

Tristan rolled his eyes. "I suppose I could take her for a walk now and then and let the lads think she prefers me still."

Clare had just a hint of a twinkle in her eye when she grinned at him. "You are very kind."

Tristan's smile was not as wide on the outside as it was on the inside. The moment Alcott said he was taking Clare back to England, Tristan made up his mind -- when she was ready to think about taking a husband, he planned to be right there waiting.

*

In a fair fight, Alcott of Cumberland, who recently became Lord of Wickerly Castle, proved to be a coward. The king granted Stuart the land he was promised -- which meant the MacGreagors had a true friend in England.

Someday they might need one.

-End-

DOLEE

CHAPTER I

She loved Camran from the depths of her very soul. She loved walking with him, talking to him and being in his arms at night. The day he asked her to marry him, Dolee floated on air and thought her feet would never touch the ground again. And since that first night, they had not been apart save for the times he went on the hunt, or Neil sent him to barter for hides from other clans. Camran MacGreagor was Dolee's whole life.

Camran's occupation was one of honor. His strong hands easily and expertly pushed the large needle and thin leather strips through the hides to make warm winter capes and coats for the clan. Sometimes he was not satisfied with his work and fretted, but on those occasions, Dolee managed to soothe him with her soft touch and her gentle tone. It made him love her even more, if it were possible.

They lived in one of the older cottages not far from the Keep, got along well with most everyone, and their little plot of land in front of the cottage was filled with Dolee's favorite flowers. When there was time, they took long walks together or went to watch the training of the young colts, which was a favorite past time of many couples. Few sights were as glorious as the prance of a strong colt with its head held high and its tail straight out.

But this year there was plenty of work and little time to watch the colts. A thick undergrowth of fur on the animals signaled a cold winter approaching and the whole clan needed to make sure they, plus the English brides were kept warm and fed. The leaves were only just beginning to turn, but some of the men felt a sense of urgency. So Neil took men away from other tasks and sent them off to hunt. When the hunt was plentiful, the women dried the extra meat and stored it just in case winter hunting became too difficult.

With Camran busy sewing, other men were sent to barter for hides. However, the MacGreagors were not the only ones to see the signs and there were few hides to be had from the other clans. Warmth, it seemed, might have to be gained by wrapping in extra plaids and keeping the hearths lit.

Therefore, the weaving of new garments and the gathering of more wood became just as important. Indeed, the days of fall were not idle days for anyone. The spinners spun the last of the wool into threads, the weavers worked their looms, the hunters went out every day, the tanners worked twice as hard as usual, and men like Camran spent nearly every waking hour sewing hides.

Dolee worried about him. His sore fingers got worse every day, but he assured her they would heal and the clan was about to run out of hides soon anyway. She tried everything to ease his discomfort including lacing his shoes and even pleated his kilt for him in the mornings. She also took over other duties, such as keeping their daggers and his sword sharpened. But in the end, all she could do was watch him work and try not to notice his discomfort.

He was not the only one hurting. Others were getting so tired they suffered more injuries than usual and Neil finally called a halt. Some of the men protested, but Neil was not willing to lose even one of them to an injury that would not heal. Instead, he removed his hold on marriages so the men could keep their beloveds warm, and began to think of other ways to conserve their resources. If the signs were true, it would be the coldest winter the MacGreagors had ever seen.

*

Camran and Dolee were perfect for each other. Both had yellow hair and blue eyes, and although his cheekbones were more pronounced and her nose was a little more pointed, they looked enough alike to be brother and sister. That happened with married couples sometimes, Dolee noticed, and speculated those were the couples who truly loved each other. It made her proud to count them among the truly in love.

Camran was never harsh or demanding and seemed content just to have her near. But their marriage was not yet perfect and although he tried to hide it, sometimes she could see the hurt in his eyes. Their love had not given him the greatest gift of all -- a son. In fact, Dolee had not given him any children.

After the first year, she began to ask for advice so often, the other women were inclined to avoid her, and nothing they suggested worked anyway. One woman told her to drink mead before she went to bed and if her stomach hurt when she woke up, it was a sign she was pregnant. Her stomach never hurt. The multitude of bitter tasting berry and herb mixtures, and other potions prescribed to help her get pregnant, did not work. Some made her so ill, Camran finally put his foot firmly down and ordered her not try any more.

The second year, Dolee consulted the priest, who was equally confounded. Most often, the women came to him asking how to keep from having children and he confessed he had little experience with a problem such as hers.

But now she was approaching the end of the third year. According to the law of the land, after three years a man could set aside his barren wife and marry another. The very thought of it made tears come to her eyes. What would she do? Where would she go and how could she ever abide knowing another woman was in his arms?

Dolee tried not to show her despair. She kept their small cottage spotless, their clothing clean and her husband well fed. She was a good wife and he often thanked her for it. But sometimes when she went to fetch a bucket of water from the river, she could not help but stop and watch the children play. The sight of them was almost as disparaging as the hurt in her husband's eyes. He was not alone in his disappointment; Dolee wanted children as much as he did.

The notion that he might be shed of her slowly grew into an obsession. She thought to ask him if he intended to set her aside, but doubted he would admit it. He did love her, she knew that for certain and therefore if he planned it, he would be forced to lie. Often, when her heart could bear the distress no longer, she excused herself and slipped into the forest to cry where he would not see.

CHAPTER II

It was on one of those quiet times in the forest that the answer came to her. For most of an hour, Dolee had been talking to God and when Nessa walked into the small clearing, she could not help but think God sent her.

The fifth from the eldest sister, Nessa was becoming more attractive every day with long dark hair and piercing blue eyes. She didn't expect to see anyone and as soon as she spotted Dolee, she stopped short. "What are you doing here?"

Dolee smiled, "Just praying for a miracle."

"Oh, forgive me for intruding." Embarrassed, she turned to go back.

"I was hoping you were my miracle."

At that, Nessa turned. "I have been called many things, but never a miracle. Edana calls me a ghost because I am too quiet, Charlotte calls me quick, Alison thinks I am witless and Aleen normally just rolls her eyes at everything I say." Nessa wrinkled her brow and then looked for a place to sit down. "Come to think of it, perhaps you could be *my* miracle."

Dolee was already seated on one of the many tree stumps available in that part of the forest and waited for Nessa to settle on one not far away. "What sort of miracle do you need?"

"I want to marry a lad who prefers another."

Dolee interlaced her fingers, laid them in her lap and thoughtfully rubbed her thumbs together. "You *do* need a miracle."

"Aye."

"Might I know who the lad is?"

"Do you promise not to tell?"

"I promise."

Nessa lightly bit her lower lip, "He is Ros and I love him dearly, but he cannot see me. Emily is always with him and she demands all his attention. She is not the right wife for him, but he is too..."

Dolee hid her smile. "Witless?"

"Precisely, too witless to know it. Oh what am I to do?"

"Well, I cannot see why you would want to marry a witless lad."

Nessa quickly stood up. "You are right. No lass wants a witless husband, even me." Just as quickly, she sat back down. "It would not do for both the husband and the wife to be witless. On the other hand, I doubt Neil would let us get too out of hand."

Dolee couldn't help but finally grin. "Tell me, what do you love about him?"

"Everything. He is strong, kind, gentle and good to his horse. A lad who is good to his horse will also be good to his wife, do you agree?"

"I do agree. If he has not noticed you, how do you know so much about his good qualities?"

"I watch him...from afar. He has three little brothers and I see the way he is with them. He is much older and one would think he is the father the way he keeps guard over them. He is never too busy to answer their questions; he takes them riding and teaches them absolutely everything he knows."

"I have noticed that too. Ros was born to his father's first wife who died. His father did not remarry for several years and thus the difference in the ages of his sons."

"I see, I did not know that. He will be a good father someday and I would give all I own to have a husband like Ros. Even his smile is kind. If only he would smile at me, but he does not. Never have I known such vexation. I have tried everything to get his attention short of kicking him in the shins."

"That would surely work." It should have made Dolee laugh, but although Nessa was helping to lighten her mood, she didn't feel like laughing just yet.

Both of them were quiet for a time, each lost in thought. Nessa took several forlorn, deep breaths and let them out. But then she studied the sadness on Dolee's face. "You are unhappy. I have seen you often looking down as though you do not want anyone to see, but I can tell you are sad. Is it your husband?"

"Not at all, he is a fine lad and I love him very much. You are young and would not understand. Perhaps…"

"I understand more than you think. Nine sisters with two lazy brothers and a stupid father makes a lass discern a great deal. Is it your lack of children?"

Dolee looked surprised. "Is it that evident?"

"Nay, it is just that you have everything else…or seem to."

"I do have everything a lass could want, save children." She forced herself to smile. "I am barren. I have tried everything and for a moment I hoped you had an answer, but now I see I was mistaken."

Nessa bit her lower lip again and tried to think of some way to help. "If only we were not so far away from the Widow Kennedy. She is a soothsayer and Edana warned us not to go there, so it is out of the question. Besides, to get there we would have to cross the land of the Kennedys. They are not so pleasant as the MacGreagors, believe me. Slava thought…"

"What could the Widow Kennedy do?"

"Well, she could tell if there is to be a child in your future. She knows all kinds of things. Edana would have my hide if she knew, but I went to see her once. Edana said mother told her soothsayers are not of God. I was very young when I went and at first, I was terrified. But the Widow Kennedy is a nice old lass who means no harm."

"How could she tell if I am to have a child?"

"Easy, she reads the stars, the fire flames, and the rings in the water when a drop falls into the bowl. I wanted to know if my mother was in heaven, you see. She read the water rings and assured me she was."

"Oh, she is a Seer. Does she have potions too?" Dolee asked.

"I saw bottles on her table, but I do not know what they are for. It is out of the question anyway, she lives very far from here and I doubt any of the men would take us. Besides, my sisters would never allow me to get that close to our old home, and without me, how would you find her?"

"You could tell me how to find her."

Nessa wrinkled her brow and thought about that for a moment. "I suppose I could. Would your husband take you?"

"He wants children as much as I do."

"You must tell him to be very careful when he crosses Kennedy land. They are not pleasant."

"Where exactly is this place?"

"Well, first you must go south and then east. The land of my father is beyond the Kennedy hold and is without many trees." She stood up, scraped dead leaves away with her foot until she got to the dirt on the ground, and then drew a map with the end of a stick. "Perhaps you should go east first and then go south until you get beyond Kennedy land."

"How will I know when I have passed Kennedy land so I may turn south?"

Nessa shook her head. "I am not sure. Perhaps you could ask for directions from one of the lasses. My father has vast herds of sheep and everyone knows him. We used to shepherd the sheep and I do not miss it one little bit. It is very hard work and the sheep are always getting lost. Edana was good at it and so was Slava, but I hated it."

"But if we find your father's home, from there where do we go?"

Nessa shifted her eyes from side to side. "Well, let me see. The widow Kennedy lives in a cottage on the top of a hill. From our land you must go farther east past the loch and I believe it is three or four hills more."

"How long will it take?"

"Two days to get there and two back, at least. Maybe more if you go around the land of the Kennedys, and of course, you must. You must avoid that clan as best you can. But Dolee, it is very, very far away."

Dolee lowered her excited eyes and stared at the ground. "I will ask my husband." Then she smiled. "About your problem, I can see no other way but to force Ros to notice you."

"You think I should kick him in the shin?"

This time Dolee's smile was genuine, "I have a better idea. First, you must watch him when he is with Emily. If they are betrothed, then you must not interfere. But if you find that he does not seem that interested in her, you should proceed."

"How do I know if he truly prefers her?"

"Watch to see if he looks into her eyes or just glances at her face. If he touches her often other than in a helpful way, then he is smitten with her. If not, then she is the one who is smitten and he is perhaps just being kind."

"And if he is just being kind, what do I do?" Nessa asked.

"Then you will be where he is as often as possible, but you must not be too obvious. When Emily is with him, go talk to her. Ask her advice, compliment her or tell her a story...anything to get his eyes away from her and on you. But be sure all your attentions are paid to her. If she suspects you are interested in him, she will not let you get near in the future."

"Do you think it will work?"

"Perhaps and perhaps not. But it is worth a try. You must be very shrewd."

"So you are saying I should ignore him?"

"Aye, talk to her, let him look at you and pretend not to notice. If he is interested, you will know soon enough." Dolee slowly stood up. "We should get back before Neil sends the lads to look for us."

"Aye." Nessa nodded and started back through the trees. "At first I did not like being so protected. It seemed someone was always coming to see to my safety. But now I find it very comforting. It is good to know that if I fall someone will soon find me and help me get home. The forest can be a frightening place in the dark."

"Indeed it can."

Nessa held a branch back until Dolee caught up with her and passed. "How old are you?"

"I am one and twenty."

"You do not look that old."

Dolee giggled. "Thank you."

"How did you know Camran was the one for you?"

"He told me so."

Nessa couldn't help but laugh. "I have not heard that one before. Were you difficult?"

"Worse, I was witless. I did not understand why he was befriending me and in the beginning, I believed that was all it was -- friendship. Now I am convinced I could not breathe without him."

CHAPTER III

As soon as they were out of the forest, Nessa hurried away to start watching Ros and Emily. But Dolee lingered and slowly walked through the glen. Perhaps God sent Nessa to her with the answer after all. It would be very odd for God to send her to a seer, if in deed soothsayers were not of God, but who was she to question God's methods?

Once that question was resolved in her mind, she began to make a plan. It was clear Camran would not take her -- he forbade her to take any more potions. None of the other men would take her either, not if Camran forbid it. She would have to go alone but she was not concerned. Dolee was a MacGreagor and she had been taught how to survive. She could indeed manage the journey all by herself and be back in four or five days at the most.

*

Just as Dolee instructed, Nessa took every precaution not to be obvious while she watched Ros with Emily. He was not holding Emily's hand and that was a good sign. However, when they turned up the path between the new cottages to walk toward the pastures, she could no longer see his face. How was she to know if he was looking into Emily's eyes or just glanced at her?

Nessa had no one to walk with and that made following them ill-mannered. She followed anyway for a little while, but Ros did not seem to look at Emily at all. They appeared to be talking, but he did not even glance Emily's direction. Another good sign, Nessa hoped.

If only she could think of something to ask Emily, but nothing came to mind. This was not going to be as easy as she thought. Exasperated, Nessa stopped, turned and went back to the courtyard.

Several of the children were playing hide and seek and when one wanted to hide behind her, she stood still. The little girl grabbed Nessa's plaid and held on long enough to peek around her. Then she rushed off to find a new hiding place. Nessa stayed for a little while longer to watch the comings and goings of others, but there was nothing very exciting to watch

She needed to go see the cobbler and since she could not watch Ros, it seemed like a good time. There was a time when the men were at her door often to ask her to walk with them, but with all the English women there now, she was not as bothered with them as before. Ros, she noticed, was never among the men wanting to court her, and perhaps that was what caught her attention.

Just outside the cobbler's cottage, she stopped short. Come to think of it, if he were betrothed to Emily she would have heard about it. There was no such thing as a secret in the MacGreagor clan.

"What?"

Nessa smiled at the aging cobbler. "Forgive me, I did not realize I was talking aloud."

"If you have come for new shoes, lass, you have come too late."

"I was afraid of that. Could you perhaps mend it?" She took hold of his arm, lifted her right foot and turned it so he could see where the stitching was coming loose on the side.

"Aye, that I can do. Come inside, sit at my table and take your shoe off."

Nessa did as she was told and then watched him work. First, he removed part of the old stitching and then dipped his needle and fine leather thread in hot beeswax so it would slide through the holes easier.

"Have you heard the news?"

"What news?" she asked.

"One of the guards heard about it and came straight away to tell Neil. The king of England executed four more lads a fortnight ago. They were accused of the murder of the old king, but some say he should have executed himself as well. Everyone suspects he was behind it. I say he has rid himself of all who might witness against him."

"Executed how?"

The cobbler looked her in the eye and then turned his attention back to his mending. "It is not for a pretty lass such as you to know how."

"Do you think the English will attack us?"

"They might try, but we will stop them. The Scots want no part of the English." He finished the last stitch, tied the knot and cut the ends. "There, that should do it."

She took the shoe, put it back on, tied the laces and stood up. "Thank you." She leaned over, put her cheek to his and then hurried out the door. Perhaps by now Ros and Emily were back where she could watch them. Besides, now she had something to talk to Emily about -- the English.

*

Dolee was being unusually quiet and Camran noticed. Now that Neil halted the work, Camran's fingers were beginning to heal and he was glad for the rest. But Dolee's silence was beginning to worry him. "What is it, love?"

She sat across from him at the table washing vegetables in a bowl of water and cutting them up to put in the pot for their evening meal. "What is what?"

"You have not said a word since you came back. Are you unwell?"

She smiled. "Nay, I am very well, save for the headache that plagues me occasionally."

"Does a harsh winter worry you?"

"A little, but I have you to keep me warm."

He put his arms on the table and leaned forward a little. "Neil says we should consider living with others if the wood begins to run short. It would be tiresome, but it is a sound idea. The clan would use only half the wood that way."

"Tiresome indeed. Will he decide with whom we are to stay or will you?"

"I will, but not without your agreement. There are some we do not get on with so well as others."

"Whom would you consider? We could stay with my brother and his family. I am certain he would welcome us."

"Aye, but you do not get along with his wife."

"I could manage it for a while. Besides, I adore my brother and he gets on well with you."

"That he does." Camran watched her set her knife down and rub her right temple. "Have you taken the medicine from the willow tree?"

"Aye, my headache should go away soon." Always when she had something on her mind, it made her head hurt and this day she had a lot to think about. She was caught in a repeating circle of wanting to go to the Widow Kennedy for help and being afraid to go alone. For a moment, she wondered just how furious her husband would be if she went against his orders. But she reasoned that if the news from the widow was good and once she told him the reason, he would forgive her.

"I could rub your back."

Dolee smiled. "Aye, but it is the middle of the day and every time you rub my back I somehow end up without my clothes on."

"But your headache goes away."

"True." He had a gleam in his eye and never had she denied him, even in the middle of the day. So she carefully set her work aside, went around the table and slipped into his lap. She kissed him and when she felt him begin to pull the back of her shirt out of her belt, she giggled. "That is how my undressing always begins."

Camran buried his head in the curve of her neck. "I can hardly rub your back any other way."

"Then your fingers do not hurt today?"

He lifted his lips to hers again and kissed her lovingly. "For you, I will bear the pain as best I can."

She giggled again and playfully smacked his arm. "For me, is it?" Then as she always did, she melted in his arms.

*

Ros and Emily were not back from their walk and Nessa found it quite annoying. She was tempted to go find them, but realized if she saw him kiss Emily, she would be devastated. It was better to wait until they came back to the courtyard. Couples rarely kissed in front of everyone in the courtyard, at least not until they were betrothed.

Nessa looked around, spotted Millin sitting outside her cottage and went to join her.

"My dear, I am happy for the company." Millin got up, went inside her cottage and came back with another chair. She waited until Nessa got settled and then sat back down. "Are you well?"

"Quite well." The courtyard was within her view and Nessa tried not to look that direction often, but couldn't seem to help herself. "Millin, you are an elder, do you fear a harsh winter?"

"I have seen a few in my years, that is for sure. We always manage to survive them even when the cold brings snow and ice to the river."

"Ice in the river? I have never seen that before. In our old home, the weather never got that cold, not that I recall."

The Widow Millin MacClurg MacGreagor noticed Nessa look toward the courtyard repeatedly, but decided not to ask. As she always did, she wore her light brown hair in one long braid down her back. Shorter unmanageable hairs broken from years of braiding framed her round face and her eyes were always kind. "There are parts of Scotland like that, I understand."

"It is true, I have only seen snow two or three times, but it melted quickly." She glanced at the courtyard again and still there was no sign of Ros or Emily. "Millin, why is it some lasses have a child every year and others do not have them so frequently? And why do some lasses have no children at all?"

Millin quickly forgave Nessa her thoughtlessness. "It seems many things in life have no answer." Nessa truly had forgotten that Millin was barren and caught her breath, but Millin reached over and patted her hand. "You meant no harm."

"I truly did not."

Millin continued, "Someday you will be asking if a lass can tell if she is to have a boy or a girl, so I might as well tell you now. Different clans have different ways, though none are completely reliable. We used to have a soothsayer living with us and she was not always right either."

"What did she do?"

"Well, she asked the lass to hold out her hand. If the lass held out her right hand, she would have a laddie and if it was her left, a lassie."

"I see, what other way is there?"

"Only one other that I am aware of. The soothsayer would bring a bowl of water and if a drop of the mother's milk floated it would be a lassie, but if it sunk she was sure to have a laddie."

Nessa wrinkled her brow. "You do not look as though you put much faith in soothsayers."

"I have only known that one, but she could get me riled like no other lass. Once I accused her of trickery, and I was right too. But my husband said to let her be."

"Trickery? What sort of trickery?"

"Oh my dear, that lass was a rogue if ever I saw one. She claimed she could tell the future by reading the bumps on a lad's head. I suppose she could by reading a palm or looking at the stars, but bumps on a head? I did not believe a word of it. On the other hand, even she had a good side. She knew how to make medicine from a plant that works very well for a toothache. She even made potions from dandelions and the waybread plants. Thank goodness she showed others how to do that before she passed. I cannot think what we would do without her cures."

CHAPTER IV

Nessa looked again toward the courtyard and began to wring her hands. Ros was looking right at her.

"Child, what is it?"

"What?" Embarrassed, Nessa quickly stood up. "Oh, it is nothing. I was just hoping to see Emily. She went for a walk with Ros and he is back." She nodded and hurried toward the courtyard. Then she abruptly stopped. Emily was nowhere in sight and Dolee said not to approach him directly.

Not only that, Nessa planned to ask Emily if she was afraid the English would attack, but realized what a stupid question it was. She turned, hung her head and soon she was staring aimlessly at the ground. She raised a hand and began to rub her forehead. There had to be a more sensible question to ask, but the harder she tried to think of one the harder it was to think at all.

"Are you lost?"

His voice was deep and strong, his smile was warm and when she looked into his eyes Nessa feared her knees would buckle. She could not remember ever being so close to Ros and he was much taller than she thought. It took all her strength, but she finally gathered her wits and returned his smile, "Aye, lost in thought. I meant to ask Emily something, but now I cannot remember what it was."

"Emily has gone home."

"It is just as well, I cannot remember what I wanted." She should say something else, Nessa believed, but then again Dolee said to ignore him. She couldn't think of anything to say anyway, so she gave him a half curtsey and started to walk away.

"Are you afraid of me?"

Amazed, Nessa stopped and turned to grin at him, "Are you afraid of me?"

He raised an eyebrow, "Then it was you who killed the lad who tried to take Alison?"

Her grin turned to a frown and she put a hand on her hip, "Why Ros MacGreagor, you know the sisters vowed not to tell. You are very brash for asking." She started to walk away again and was surprised when he began to walk beside her.

"You will not tell even me?"

"And why should I tell you and none other?"

"Because I am the most curious. I lay awake nights trying to figure it out, you see."

Nessa tried not to smile. "Well, I could hardly keep a lad from his rest."

"Then you will tell me?"

"Nay."

"If I guess correctly, then will you tell me?" he asked.

"Nay."

"Perhaps bribery then. I will take you riding … twice. I will build you a cottage and I will hunt just for you."

That made her stop walking and turn to stare at him. "How many nights has it been since you slept?"

Ros laughed. Then he pulled the tie out and let his blond hair fall down around his shoulders. Still grinning, he held the tie up in front of her face. "This was a gift from my mother. It is yours to keep and all you need do is tell me your secret."

It was an ordinary length of wool string and Nessa rolled her eyes. "Your mother did not love you, did she?"

He lowered the string and pretended to pout. "You will not tell anyone about my mother, will you?"

"You want me to keep yet another secret? I will go daft."

He put his hands behind his back and started them walking again. "Do you know, you are the only one in the clan with a secret of any consequence, you and your sisters that is."

"It is a dreadful burden, but we manage. Hopefully, we will not have to do that again...kill a lad, I mean. We are not fond of killing, but when there was just the nine of us, we had little choice. Now we have all of you to protect us."

"You had all of us that night too. Why did you not let the lads rescue her?"

She folded her arms and looked away. "We did not trust you."

He was surprised by her honesty. "And now? Do you trust us now?"

"I do, although I admit it has taken these many months. Some things come natural when taught at an early age, and we were carefully taught to protect each other from the time we learned to walk." Now that she had seen him up close, she thought him even more handsome, particularly with his hair let loose. Being so close made her sorry she was almost home.

"Most lasses find it difficult to learn to kill."

"They would not hesitate to protect those they love. Being alert is learned, killing is something…"

"That happens without thought?"

"Aye, without any thought at all. The moment comes and the killing is done before one has time to think about it."

"But later, you think about it constantly until it mercifully fades into a memory."

"You have killed a lad?"

He did not hesitate to answer, "Aye."

"Do you wish to tell me?"

"Nay, it was a long time ago and best forgotten. Still, it is good to talk with someone who can truly understand."

Too soon she was home and standing in front of the cottage she shared with her younger sisters. "I am fortunate to have nine sisters who truly understand." He did not seem to want to leave and she did not know what more to say, so she just stood there staring at the ground. He was finally looking at her and as Dolee instructed, she let him.

"Nessa, what frightens you?"

"A wild boar. I have only seen a few, but I have yet to see anything more terrifying. Why do you ask?"

"I was just curious." With that, he nodded and walked back down the path to the courtyard.

A few moments later, he was out of sight and Nessa was left wondering what that was all about. Why did he want to know what frightened her?

She frowned and turned the question over and over in her mind.

Perhaps he and Emily planned to frighten her with a boar's head as a jest, although she could not think why they would go to the trouble. Emily was nice enough, but the two women had not spent a lot of time together. With nine sisters, Nessa hardly had time to spend with any of the other young women. She slowly turned around and opened the door. Perhaps he was just curious as he said.

*

For the second time in a few months, Ben quietly entered the Keep to wait for Neil to wake up. The sunrise promised good weather, not the crisp air that signaled winter. He again admired the colorful, stuffed pillows along the walls, the smell of the burning embers in the hearth and took a moment to get a close look at the sword that once belonged to Laird Kevin MacGreagor, a man he greatly loved and remembered from his childhood. Then Ben quietly sat down at the table and waited for Neil to come down the stairs. The news he had this day was not good and his concern was evident on his face.

"What?" Neil asked, suddenly appearing in the doorway and then walking across the great hall to the table.

"Two horses missing." Ben quickly got to his feet so he could look his laird in the eye."

"They might have wandered away."

"Nay, both were tied to a tree awaiting the morning guards."

Neil lowered his eyes and ran his fingers through his tousled hair. "Have you any idea how long they have been gone?"

"Two, maybe three hours. I remember seeing them when the moon was still high and it is down now. We gained a new colt in the night and I did not check on the horses."

"Were they packed with provisions?"

"Aye, just as they always are and I have already sent lads to look for them. Perhaps I did not tie them well enough."

"That would surprise me. For years, you have been preparing horses for the morning guards and never have you been remiss. The Haldane were spotted in the woods yesterday, perhaps they are thieves. The Haldane trouble me, they say not a word to any of us and it is unsettling. Perhaps it is time to pay them a visit."

Ben kept quiet and just let Neil talk. On this subject, he did not feel qualified to offer advice and instead waited to be discharged. But Neil did not send him back to the animals, even when Walrick, Gelson and several of the other men came in to await the orders that would start their day. Each man was told the news immediately upon entering and each frowned. Missing horses were always a great concern.

Glenna brought Justin and the baby down, the serving women began to serve their morning meal and the men began to discuss the situation. Such a gathering so early always made Glenna smile. The men could not help but watch her eat and if Neil would let them, they would have one morning meal in the cottage with their wives and another in the Keep with them. Some of the men, she feared never managed to quench their abundant appetites no matter how much they ate.

Normally she ignored the men as they talked. Instead, she kept an eye out to be sure enough food was sent to the middle floor, where some of Walrick's adopted children yet resided. Then she turned her attention to considering how many could live on all three floors, should the winter be as cold as they feared.

On the other hand, it took considerable wood and perhaps trying to keep such a large building warm was not the best way to conserve. If the families doubled up and even tripled in the smaller cottages, they would use only one third of the wood. But when should they begin to share provisions? And what if they did not begin soon enough? It was not an easy question to answer.

Normally there was nothing fascinating in what the men had to say, but when Camran bolted through the door, everyone looked up including Glenna.

He nearly shouted, "I cannot find Dolee." Camran's face was pale, his hair tousled and his kilt haphazardly tucked under his belt. "She was gone when I woke up. She built no fire in the hearth as she always does and I have looked everywhere."

CHAPTER V

Neil shoved his bowl away and stood up. "We have two horses missing also." He glanced at Walrick but gave his orders to all the men. "Find her. Wake everyone up and see if anyone else is missing, then search the woods." In an instant, the men filed out and scattered in all directions, each wanting to assure himself that his family was accounted for before they began the search.

Walrick headed upstairs, made sure his children were there and then headed off to fetch Steppen. Whatever was to come, he would be happier if Steppen was in the Keep with Glenna.

With the great hall suddenly empty except for her small family, Glenna remained quiet and let her husband think. For the sake of two stolen horses, he would not go to war, but for a woman -- aye, her beloved husband would fight to the death if anyone took one of the women.

The children were finally fed and she was no longer hungry, but still she did not go back upstairs. Instead, Glenna played with the baby and watched Neil pace in front of the hearth.

*

Camran knew not where to go or what to do, so he stood alone in the courtyard facing one direction, and then turned to face another. He too was terrified someone had taken his wife and he would surely kill the scunner, if he could manage to figure out whom it was. But for now, his heart was filled with terror. Was she hurt, was she this moment being forced, was she dead? He brought his hands up and covered his eyes. She can't be dead -- he would not let her be dead.

Walrick was the first one back and brought Steppen with him. He immediately went to Neil and she went to sit by Glenna at the table. "The two might not be connected," Walrick said.

"I have considered that. But if a lad came in the night on foot, he might take two horses to carry her off."

"If a lad came to take her away, he would only need one horse and the better to keep her quiet if he had her on his horse."

"True, but both are possible. He might have pulled the other horse behind him."

"Or someone stole two horses and Dolee just got lost in the forest."

Neil grabbed his friend's upper arms. "I pray that is exactly what happened. Send the men who were on guard last night to me. Someone must have seen something." He expected Walrick to leave straight away, but when he didn't Neil waited for him to speak.

"Camran is standing in the courtyard befuddled."

"Bring him in here. She is his wife and he has a right to know what is happening." But instead of waiting for Walrick to do it, Neil went out and got him. He brought Camran in, led him to the table and was about to tell him to sit down when he noticed his disheveled kilt. "Have you forgotten how to dress yourself?" Neil meant it as a jest, but as soon as Camran turned his hands over and showed his injured fingers, Neil slumped. "Forgive me."

Neil sat down at the table, waited for the women to turn so they were facing away from them and pulled some of the pleats out of

Camran's belt. Then he expertly began to put them back. "When my father was near the end of his life, I often pleated his kilt. It is not as easy as it seems for it is backwards, you see." He glanced up at Camran's attempt to smile. "We will find her. We will not rest until she is back in your arms, I swear it." He finished and stood back up.

"Thank you." Camran did not know if he should leave again so he waited.

Neil, on the other hand was well aware that Camran needed something to do. But with his injured hands, a task would not be so easily found.

Glenna motioned for Camran to sit down at the table. "Perhaps you might teach Justin how to count. As soon as he is more fully awake, he will be chattering away. It would be a great favor to me if he had you to answer all his questions." The nod of appreciation Glenna got from her husband warmed her heart. Feeling useful for something other than bearing children was important to her.

*

Outside, Gelson began giving orders. He sent men to walk along the riverbank in case she fell in. Others gave the village a thorough search, walking down every path and looking between the cottages. But the bulk of the men fanned out and disappeared into the forest on opposite sides of the glen. The night guards had not seen her or anything suspicious, and as soon as they reported it to Neil, they joined in the search.

*

There was an eerie silence as most of the women stood outside their cottages and listened to an occasional far off man shouting

Dolee's name. As the time went by, they drifted back inside. The children still had to be fed, the animals needed tending and there were chores to be done. And when they happened to be together, they speculated on what had happened, and who might be to blame in soft tones just above a whisper.

Some of the women were near tears as the morning turned toward afternoon. Others were beginning to get angry at the thought that someone might have taken her.

Most of the men were getting angry too. The longer they searched the more likely it seemed that someone had taken her and war was on every man's mind. Still they searched, looking between trees and behind bushes just in case she was unwell and passed out somewhere. But Dolee had simply vanished and by the noon meal, the men began to come back to the hold to collect a meal and mount their horses.

Camran spent the morning going out to look for her and then coming back several minutes later to see if anyone had found her. It was making everyone daft, but none of them knew how to help him or what they would do in his position. They only thanked God it was not their wife, mother or daughter who was missing.

*

Ros returned from searching to find both Emily and Nessa in the courtyard, although they were on opposite sides. Emily smiled and was happy to see him, but Nessa didn't notice his return and he found that disappointing. Instead, she was standing near the rock wall, staring down the path toward the pasture. He ignored Emily and went to Nessa. "Are you lost again?"

But this time when she turned to look at him, there were tears forming in the bottom of her eyes. Alarmed, he took hold of her arms and turned her to face him. "What is it?"

"Nothing."

"You do not strike me as the kind of woman who cries for nothing. Is it Dolee? I saw you talking to her yesterday."

"You saw us? Did you hear what we were talking about?"

"Nay, what were you talking about?"

"Nothing important."

She would not look at him, which convinced Ros she was hiding something. "If you know where she is, you must tell us."

"I thought they would find her by now, but...Neil will send me away and I will not blame him if he does."

"I have never known Neil to banish a good lass. Why would he send you away?"

The tears clouded her eyes again and she hung her head. "I did not mean to, but I have done something wrong."

Ros did not wait for her full confession. Instead, he grabbed her hand, pulled her across the courtyard and then through the door of the Keep. He had her standing directly in front of Neil before he let go of her hand.

Nessa began to sob. "It is my fault."

Neil wrinkled his brow, "What is your fault?"

"It is my fault Dolee is missing."

"How could it be your fault?"

"Please do not banish me."

Neil lifted her chin with his hand and made her look at him. "I will not banish you unless you have killed her. Have you killed her?"

"Nay, I swear it!"

"I thought not, but you do know where she is?"

Nessa accepted the cloth Steppen handed her and dried the tears on her cheeks. "She has gone to see the Widow Kennedy."

"The soothsayer?" A very pregnant Edana hurried to stand right behind her sister. "Nessa, what have you done?"

CHAPTER VI

Nessa quickly turned to face the eldest of her sisters. Always when the sisters confronted her, it made her mind go blank and she struggled to find the words. "I did not think…she wants a child and I said the Widow Kennedy might be able to help. I told her not to go…at least I think I told her not to go. I truly did caution her to stay clear of the Kennedys."

The great hall was quickly filling with sisters, who seemed to magically know where the others were at all times. Said Charlotte, "Did you tell her how to find the Widow Kennedy?"

"I might have." Nessa backed up a step nearly running into Neil. "I believe I did, come to think of it. But she said her husband would take her. I did not know she would go alone. How could I know that?" When she looked, Alison mouthed the word, "witless" and Aleen rolled her eyes.

It was Neil who turned Nessa back around to face him. "You will tell us where the Widow Kennedy lives."

"Nay, I will take you there," said Slava.

Neil looked at her and then at each of the married sisters, the oldest of whom had the swell of a child at various stages. Nessa was now the eldest unmarried woman and the logical choice. "Nessa will take the lads."

The sisters wanted to object, but Neil was right and if they went now, the men might quickly catch up with Dolee and be back the next day. Reluctantly, Edana nodded and gathered Nessa in her arms. Then she walked her sister out the door. "You best take my dagger, it is the sharpest. You will also need…"

*

Twenty men, including Camran and Ros, whom Neil chose to lead them, were waiting for Nessa when Neil lifted her onto her horse and handed her the reins. "Godspeed."

She nodded, said, "Whoa," to her horse, which caused the horse to go forward, and then smiled at the stunned look on the face of one of the men standing in the courtyard. "Ask my sisters to explain."

They rode to the end of the valley and then just as Nessa instructed Dolee, they turned east. It did not take but a few hours for Nessa to see the futility of the search. The men spread out as far as they dared and still the amount of land they were able to cover was relatively small. Dolee could be anywhere -- down in a valley, up on a hill or one mile over in any direction.

Searching east offered the more difficult terrain with steeper hills and abrupt cliffs. Occasionally, they stopped to examine the dirt for tracks, but even when they did find some, they did not look fresh.

If Dolee heeded Nessa's advice and went east, how far east would she go before she turned south? Nessa remembered drawing a map of sorts in the dirt, but she did not say -- when you see this or that, turn south.

All they could do was look for a sign that Dolee had passed that way and there simply was no sign. The men spread out, drew in close together in the narrower parts of the meadows or valleys and spread out again, each taking a section of land and each watching the ground for something -- anything that might tell them Dolee had come that way.

Ros occasionally glanced at a worried Camran, but there was little he could say or do to reassure the man. They dared not call her name for fear they might draw the wrong kind of attention to Dolee. So for the most part they just followed Nessa, kept an eye out for warriors from other clans and searched.

By the time they stopped for the night, Nessa was exhausted. She spread her plaid by the small campfire, sat down, pulled the bread Edana packed for her out of her sack and began to nibble. As soon as Ros sat down on his plaid not far away, she looked at him. "Dolee might have ignored my advice and gone straight across the Kennedy hold. If she came this way we would have caught up with her by now."

"She had a good head start, we will find her tomorrow."

Nessa nodded, but she blamed herself. If she had gone to Neil sooner, they surely would have found Dolee by now. She took another bite of bread, wrapped it back up in the cloth and then put it back in her sack. It seemed to take the last of her strength to chew and swallow. Her eyes drooped and her head fell forward just before Ros caught her arm, helped her lay down, and then covered her with her extra plaid.

*

The next thing she knew, it was morning and Camran was shaking her awake. "It is cloudy."

She tried, but could not quite understand. "What?"

"It is cloudy and Dolee has no sense of direction. We must find her soon or she will be lost to us forever."

Nessa quickly sat up and began to gather her things. She tried not to notice the terror in Camran's eyes or the concern on the faces of the other men. She let Ros help her on her horse, but did not wait for him to mount before she urged her horse onward. If Camran felt it was urgent, then she felt it too.

Two hours went by before they stopped on the crest of a hill to see if they could spot Dolee. Nessa slid down off her horse. It felt good to stretch her legs and she too searched the land below with her eyes until Ros came to stand beside her. "Why do you think she took two horses?"

"I find it comforting that she did. Both had provisions and knowing she has food and water is a comfort," he answered.

"I did tell her it would take at least two days going and two coming back. Perhaps she thought she would need that much." Nessa turned to look in another direction. The trees were not as thick in this part of the forest and over the tops she could see a range of far off mountains. "I am so frightened for her and I fear finding her is hopeless."

He wanted to hold her and give her his strength, but this was not the time or the place. "It is not hopeless and you must not think it. Camran will see if you give up and you must be strong for his sake."

"You are right, of course. I recognize those mountains and we should turn south now. The Kennedys will not bother us here."

*

Nessa was wrong and more than once, the MacGreagors hid in

the woods to let a band of Kennedy warriors pass by. Then the MacGreagors moved on. Again they searched and again they saw nothing. But the terrain was beginning to look more familiar to Nessa and it was a relief to know she was leading them in the right direction. She did not say so, but the thought of getting them all lost weighed heavy on her mind. Now she could relax a little. By afternoon, the clouds drifted away and Camran seemed relieved, which also helped her relax.

When they stopped again, she knelt at the edge of a stream and splashed water on her face. Then she cupped her hands, drank and dried her face with her cloth. It was exactly the kind of refreshment she needed.

Camran had been quite for most of the day, but there was a question on his mind, "Nessa, do you believe the widow Kennedy could truly tell Dolee if she were to have children?"

She stood up and turned to look at Dolee's husband. "I did, but not after Millin explained it to me."

Camran offered his hand and helped her walk over the rocks until she was away from the stream. "What did Millin say?"

"Well, I was very young when I went to see the widow Kennedy. After my mother passed, I wanted to be certain she was in heaven. Widow Kennedy read the water rings and assured me she was. But Millin says a soothsayer can make the rings say whatever the person wants to hear. Who would know the difference?"

Camran nodded. "Millin is right."

"I see that now." Suddenly she did not know what to say. She thought to apologize again, but he surely did not want to hear it. She thought to offer some words of hope, but she feared he might find her feeble attempt insincere. So when he walked away, she let him go without a word and felt guilty for doing it. If only she could take back everything she told Dolee.

*

Nessa was paying very little attention to him, but Ros kept a close eye on her. Besieged by each of the sisters before they left, he faithfully promised to bring her back safe and sound. But that was not the reason for his attentions. She was perhaps not the most beautiful of the sisters, but she was by all accounts the most intelligent and he liked her…he liked her a lot.

When the sisters first came to live with the MacGreagor Clan they were constantly surrounded by men wanting their attention, so Ros did not even try. One by one the elder sisters married and then the English brides arrived and Nessa's attention was not in such demand. But getting her to pay attention to him was more of a chore than he realized until a month ago. Finally, she seemed to realize he was alive and now they were together, often riding side by side, albeit for a very unhappy reason. On a more fitting occasion, he would have been pleased indeed.

He did not show it, but he was as unsettled by not having found Dolee by now as Nessa was. And as concerned as he was for Dolee, he was beginning to worry almost as much about the growing despair in Nessa's eyes. It was easy to see she blamed herself and there was little he could do about it.

Not good at concealing her feelings, Nessa's expressions gave her thoughts away and Ros had learned in just a short time when she needed to stop. But she would not allow him to stop for her often and instead kept them moving. She was determined Dolee was not going to die just because she was tired. By the time they halted for the second night and the men began to fall asleep around the campfire, she was so distraught and weary, all she seemed able to do was stare into the embers of the fire.

Her eyes were shifting and Ros feared she was going over all the horrible things that might have happened to Dolee, so he tried to distract her. "Do you miss your father and brothers?"

She looked at him and rolled her eyes, "Does a cow miss a pesky fly?" She enjoyed the laughter in his eyes and smiled. "We cannot be very far away from my father's home now."

"Are you afraid of them?"

"Nay, they are afraid of us. However, I would not wish to see my father again or talk to my brothers. They sold us, you know."

"I heard that."

"Slade found us, brought us to the MacGreagors and we are happy. I do not believe our lives would be half so good, if Slade had not agreed to take us with him that day in the woods."

"Can you sleep now?" Just as he hoped, distracting Nessa helped and when she nodded and then turned to stretch out on her plaid, he covered her and stayed until she was asleep.

Even in her sleep, the worry lines did not completely leave her brow.

CHAPTER VII

Morning did not come so early, nor was Nessa awakened so urgently as the day before. On this morning, the sky was again clear and the directions were easy to discern by the placement of the sun. Dolee would be able to tell east from west even if she happened to get turned around. The question was, did she happen to get so turned around the day before, that she went a considerable distance in the wrong direction altogether?

Suddenly, Scotland was way too big.

Again, they searched, again there was no sign of Dolee. They were traveling well out of the forest and into the relatively barren land of Nessa's youth. As they rode past the cottage, the sheds and the corrals of her father, Nessa saw no one at all and the sheep and cattle were gone. She breathed easer and moved on without pointing it out to any of the men. It was a life happily left behind. She thought about stopping to put flowers on her mother's grave, but she decided against it. The last thing Camran needed was to look upon a grave.

The MacGreagors rounded the loch, and the number of hills from the loch to the Widow Kennedy's house numbered only two instead of three or four. But there were no horses tied in front of the cottage and the old woman sat alone in a chair outside.

The sight of twenty men wearing unfamiliar plaids might frighten the old woman, Nessa thought, so she slipped down off her horse and walked the rest of the way up the hill alone. Though still alert of mind, the widow looked considerably older than Nessa remembered. Her cottage was aged and weather beaten, which was something Nessa had not noticed before.

Nessa spoke to her in soft tones and then did the hardest thing she had ever had to do -- she turned to look at Camran, shook her head and watched him lower his eyes. The Widow Kennedy had not seen Dolee. In fact, she had not seen another human being in a fortnight. Nessa thanked her, promised to come back again someday and then walked back down the hill.

Her heart hurt for Camran but when she returned to the men and remounted her horse, she hid her feelings. "That loch we passed has a good number of fish begging to be caught. Perhaps we got ahead of her. Perhaps we should stay at least until morning and wait for her."

Slowly, Camran nodded. He followed Nessa back to the loch, dismounted and then aimlessly looked out across the water. He tried not to think the worst, but even he knew the longer it took to find his wife, the less likely she was still alive. The men tried to get him interested in fishing, but he declined and walked to the top of a nearby hill to see if he could spot her. Too soon, the sun would set.

Nessa watched him from below, hoping for a shout or a signal of some kind. So intense were her hopes, she did not notice that Ros was standing right beside her again, where he always seemed to be. She had not forgotten her attraction to him, but she had set it aside. Yet when she finally noticed, his nearness sent unexpected excitement through her veins.

"It is not your fault," Ros said.

Nessa let out a forgotten breath and closed her eyes, "Why did she do it? She said she would have her husband take her."

"Dolee kept taking potions that made her sick and Camran forbid her to take any more. She was well aware he would not bring her."

"Then it *is* my fault. She asked if the Widow Kennedy had bottles and I said she did, though I did not know what they were for."

"You could not have known she would go alone."

"Nay, but if I had not mentioned this place she would not have tried to find it. Alison is right, I am witless."

Said Ros, "All brothers and sisters think the others are witless."

Nessa was not really listening. Instead, she watched Camran finally give up looking and bow his head. It made her want to cry. "Is there no way to ease his pain?"

"If there were, I would have done it by now."

"Dolee loves him very much, she told me so."

"Perhaps later you should tell him that. He might need to hear her words if we do not find her."

Nessa finally took her eyes off Camran and turned to Ros. "We will not stop looking, will we?"

"We will not and you need not worry about that. When we go back, we will go straight and we will find her."

"I do so pray you are right." Nessa allowed herself just a moment to look deep into his eyes, then she walked back to take her sack off her horse, open it and spread her plaid.

The men who fished caught enough to feed them, men built a fire and tended the cooking while still others took turns standing guard. They were out in the open with no trees to hide behind, but at least they could see someone coming from a good distance away.

Nessa tried to relax so she could sleep, but when the fire began to diminish, she got worried and got back up. She looked for Ros, spotted him talking to the guards and hurried to him. "You must build a bigger fire and keep it burning all night."

Ros started to ask where she suggested they get that much wood in this barren land, but then noticed the look of terror in her eyes. "Are you afraid the Kennedys will find us?"

"Nay, I am worried a wild boar will."

"I see."

"I doubt you do. They are common in this part of Scotland and not to be ignored."

"And they are the thing you fear most in the world."

"Aye."

"Nessa, we are twenty men capable of protecting you even from a wild boar." She did not look convinced and when she started to wring her hands, he took hold of them to stop her. "I will alert the lads and if it pleases you, I will put my bed next to yours. You will be safe."

Nessa pulled her hands away and went back to her bed. She doubted they understood the danger, but there was little she could do about it. A man, even a brave man could not fully understand until he was actually face to face with an angry and determined wild boar. For the first time, she was grateful Dolee had not made it this far for she forgot to warn her about the wild boars.

*

She did not think she would sleep, but when Nessa awoke the next morning, Ros was sleeping next to her as he promised. To her relief, the wild boars stayed away and to her sorrow, Dolee was yet to be found.

They packed up their things, mounted and headed into the land of the Kennedys. Again, they passed the place of her birth and this time Nessa marveled at how small their cottage was. How on earth had so many people managed to live in there?

As they had before, the men spread out and looked for signs of Dolee -- broken branches, tracks and God forbid blood. With each passing hour, Camran looked older and even more pale. Nessa tried not to watch him but now that she was not leading them any longer, Camran was in front of her and she could not help but see when he slumped or took a deep breath. It was breaking her heart into tiny pieces, but she vowed not to cry. This was neither the time nor the place for self-pity.

By the noon meal it was not Camran or Dolee Ros was most worried about. Nessa barely slept the night before, did not want to eat and seemed constantly on the verge of tears. Losing one woman was more than enough to his way of thinking, so when she went off by herself for her comfort, he ordered the men to quicken their pace.

Camran ate the last bite of bread he brought with him and then turned to Ros. "Take her back; there is no need for her to be here now. I will stay behind and look for Dolee."

Ros was not surprised when most of the men agreed to stay behind with Camran. He nodded and when Nessa came back, he explained they would be splitting up. He did not elaborate on why and was grateful she did not ask. They both now believed finding Dolee was hopeless, but neither wanted to say it out loud.

She hugged Camran, wished the men staying behind well and let

Ros and two other men take her toward home. But Nessa could not stop thinking about the missing woman. Suppose Dolee's horses got loose in the night and wandered off. She could be on foot and the forest held so many hiding places a hundred men could not see them all. Even if she still had the horses, she might have seen men wearing unfamiliar plaids, got upset and was afraid to continue on. Perhaps she fell and broke a leg, perhaps the horse threw her, or she was ill, or a man with immoral intentions got to her.

Nessa could certainly see how Neil's edict forbidding the women to go anywhere alone was a good one. Dolee was simply gone and no one would ever come to tell them what happened to her. They might never, ever know and as hard as she tried, Nessa could not shake her fears and imaginings.

Finally, Ros insisted they stop in a small meadow to rest the horses. As soon as she dismounted, she led her horse to a creek, let him drink his fill and then held on to the reins while he grazed on the tall grass. It was a peaceful little meadow which she found comforting. But too soon, Ros got them headed home again.

Ros was worried about her. She had not said a word and even when they stopped for the night, she was quiet. Then her mood seemed to brighten a little and she looked at him with hope in her eyes.

"Perhaps she is not lost at all. Perhaps Neil found her and is waiting for us to come home."

Ros nodded. If it pleased Nessa to think that, then it pleased him. At least she seemed to be a little less upset now that she was not constantly watching Camran. Still, when he offered her some barley oats to eat, she again was not hungry and it concerned him. "Nessa, you must eat. If I do not bring you back healthy, your sisters will do me in."

Nessa smiled for the first time in two days. "You should just surrender immediately. It will be less painful that way."

"I surrendered more than a week ago, you just have not yet noticed."

"I do not understand."

"I did not think you did. Come with me and I will show you." He enjoyed the perplexed look on her face. She truly had no idea what he was about to do. As soon as he got her out of sight of the other two men, he stopped, put his arms around her, drew her to him and kissed her.

But Nessa resisted and pulled away. "What are you doing?"

"I am kissing you."

"Well I know that, but you cannot."

"Why not?"

"Because you are...I mean, what about Emily?"

"Oh." He let go and moved away. "That means you have noticed me."

"Of course I have noticed you, but you are always with Emily and I thought..."

"She is not here now."

"Nay, she is not, but I wish she were. I do not...what I mean is, if she prefers you, I would not want to hurt her."

"That is very kind of you."

Nessa rolled her eyes. "You are not taking me seriously."

"If a lad loves a lass, should he let her marry someone who does not love her as much?"

Nessa turned and started to walk away, but he grabbed her hand and pulled until she turned back to face him. "I am too tired for riddles."

He pulled her back into his arms and instead of kissing her, he just held her close. "I know, do forgive me."

His arms offered the kind of strength she needed most just now and she welcomed it. She wanted to stay there and was grateful he did not demand more conversation. But it also reminded her of how tired she was and when he took her back to the others so she could sleep, she went willingly.

Nessa slept, but fitfully. Twice a frightening nightmare woke her and with her mind so plagued, it took a long time to go back to sleep.

CHAPTER VIII

The whistles echoing down the glen signaled their return, but there would be no joyous reunion. Instead, the four searchers were greeted with silence from the men and tears in the eyes of the women. Nor did Neil come to tell them Dolee had been found and was well. After nearly a week of worry and despair, Nessa could no longer hold back her tears.

As soon as they reached the courtyard, Ros got off his horse and went to Nessa. He lifted her down, but he did not let go. Instead, he scooped her up in his arms and headed for the cottage she shared with her younger sisters.

Then he felt her grab hold of his shirt, bury her head in his shoulder and begin to sob. He stopped, leaned his head against the top of hers and just let her cry. Surrounded by words of comfort from her sisters, at last, she pulled herself together and he took her on home. He paused to wait while Aleen opened the door, then he carried her inside and laid her on the nearest bed. Even then, he did not leave. Instead, he knelt down next to the bed and held her hand. "Do you want me to stay until you are asleep?"

He smiled when she nodded and in just a few minutes, she drifted off. He watched Aleen spread a plaid over her sister, brushed a strand of hair off her forehead and then went outside where he knew Neil was waiting.

"How is she?" Neil asked.

Ros waited to answer until all the sisters were gathered around him. "She blames herself. She stopped eating two days ago and has slept little, although she has not cried until just now."

"Was there no sign of Dolee?" asked Neil.

"We saw nothing. The rest of the lads stayed with Camran to keep searching, but he thought it best to bring Nessa back and I agreed. Have you heard anything?"

I sent inquires to the other clans and those that reported back say they have not seen her." Neil folded his arms and kept his voice low. "You have done the best you can, go to your rest."

*

Ros tried to rest, but he was worried and after bathing in the loch, he went back to see about Nessa. To his surprise, she was awake and all eight of her sisters were insisting she eat. She balked, protested and whined, until she realized the only way to shut them up was to eat. It made Ros smile and when she spotted him in the doorway, she glared. No longer worried, he back out of the door and left. Nessa's sisters would see to her.

But for the next two days, the sisters would not let him see her. They said she was resting, or bathing or sleeping, none of which he believed. Had he done something wrong? Was she rejecting him? Lost in thought, he headed down the path to the end of the new cottages.

The whistles began again at the bottom of the glen and everyone gathered to watch. It had to be Camran and the men, whom they prayed, had a very alive and very healthy Dolee with them. But the closer they got the more evident it was the search had been unsuccessful.

At length, Ros hung his head and close his eyes. But then he felt a hand take his and when he looked, Nessa was standing beside him with tears in her eyes. He dropped her hand, put his arm around her and together they watched Camran slide down off his horse and walk up the path to the cottage he once shared with his wife. Camran opened the door, went inside and softly closed the door behind him.

"I cannot bear it," Nessa whispered.

"Nor can the rest of us." He took her hand again and started to walk her down the glen toward the horses.

"I should take him something to eat."

"Dolee's brother will see to him," he said.

"I did not know she had a brother."

"Most of the MacGreagors are related in one way or another. Emily is my cousin."

Nessa hesitated to ask, but she had to know. "Will you marry her?"

Ros stopped walking and turned to face her. "I am not holding her hand, I am holding yours. Emily and I have been friends all our lives. She loves me and I love her very much, but not in the way you think."

"But you are with her constantly."

"And you are with your sisters constantly. That is the way of families."

"Then you are not going to marry Emily?"

"Only if you deny me."

Nessa finally smiled, "Are you asking, Ros MacGreagor."

"I am."

She let him wrap both arms around her. "Then you are not afraid of me?"

"I am afraid you will not marry me."

"I cannot refuse."

He lightly kissed her lips. "Why not?"

"Because I am not willing to let Emily have you."

His smile grew wide and he lightly kissed her lips again. "Is that a yea, Nessa MacGreagor?"

She did not answer, instead she got lost in his kiss and the feel of his arms.

*

The minutes, the hours and the days passed without any word of Dolee, but at least no one found blood, bones or remnants of a MacGreagor plaid. It was not much, but it was some measure of hope to hang on to.

Camran and two others went once more to look for her and came back within a week. In his heart, he believed she was still alive somewhere and forbid himself to mourn the loss of her. It would be like giving up. Just the same, his heart was heavy and his concentration poor.

Doing nothing caused the time to endlessly drag on and he found himself using the scraps of hides to make little covers for the children. He ate, slept and worked so he would not have to think about his missing wife.

Then winter came.

When the clan awoke, the morning dew was frozen and the air was cold. Camran walked to his door, opened it and gazed out. Was Dolee warm enough? It was one more plague on his soul, and he wondered just how much torture his mind could withstand before he went daft. Then he supposed going daft would be far more pleasant than what he was feeling currently.

Slowly he closed the door and began to play the game he now played every waking moment - when Dolee comes home, everything must be ready. There must be food, water and ample warmth. For Dolee's sake, he retrieved a candle from the table, lit the fire in the hearth and gently fanned the flames with his hand.

Winter was indeed unkind. What began with one frosty morning turned to thick dark clouds, ice around the edges of the lakes, and then the snow began to fall. Certain the other clans would not be out and about either, Neil kept fewer men outside and those that were, stayed close to the cottages so they could go inside and get warm occasionally.

To preserve wood, Neil advised everyone to double up. Walrick, Steppen and all their adopted children stayed on the second floor of the Keep, while Gelson and his family let their cottage grow cold and sought warmth with Neil and his family in the great hall. They left the third floor empty. Three days later, Neil sent word to double up again and several more families came, including the sisters, Jessup, Kadick, their husbands and some of the English brides. Ros came often to see Nessa so Neil finally let him stay.

It might have been a party atmosphere had it not been so cold. There was little to do but tell stories. The sisters told of life with their father, Glenna talked of her mother knocking the air out of her father, and before long, the stories were growing longer and more detailed.

Most doubted all of it was true. Every hour, Neil and Walrick went outside to check the weather, the wood supply and the guards.

During the next two days, the cloudy skies delivered still more snow until it was so deep, it measured mid-calf on Neil's leg. The men went out each day to break the ice on the loch, so the animals could drink, and to dip their buckets and haul water for the clan. Baths were out of the question.

The wood was dwindling but not at an alarming rate. They had enough food and so far, none were unwell save Camran who now had nothing to do but mourn his missing wife. Dolee's brother and his wife tried their best, but it was clear nothing except Dolee's arms were going to console him. Then when Camran asked Neil for a turn at standing guard, Neil saw it as a sign he was doing better.

The days passed slowly and still the MacGreagors waited for the dark clouds to lift and the air to warm.

Finally, sunlight filtered once more through the heavily draped windows, the snow began to melt and clansmen took their families home. Children ventured out and mothers were so glad to get them out from under foot, they did not care about all the muddy messes that would need cleaning later. Then the mud turned back to dry dirt, the air warmed significantly and life began to return to normal.

For Camran, going back home where he could once more prepare everything for Dolee's return seemed to ease his grief. He refused to lose hope. He simply loved her too much to let go.

CHAPTER IX

It was Ben who saw them first. He and two of the other men were feeding the horses in the corral when he happened to glance down the valley. They were definitely horses, two in all, but he could not see a rider. He thought he recognized them as the missing horses, but he was not quite certain, so he just watched as they came closer and closer.

Suddenly, Ben caught his breath. He took hold of the rope he laid over the fence earlier and grabbed a small bag of grain. Then he climbed up the side of the fence, went over the top and hopped down. Afraid he would spook the unbridled horses, he put the rope over his shoulder, reached in his bag and withdrew a handful of grain hoping to tempt the horses to come to him. It worked. As soon as he held out his hand, both horses quickened their pace and came. He let both have a taste, grabbed the rope and put the noose over the head of the larger of the two horses.

The bulge atop the horse was covered by a cowhide coat and hardly looked like it held a human being inside. But the bare foot hanging down was unmistakably that of a woman -- it was without color which made Ben certain she was not still alive.

Slade was the second to arrive and quickly took hold of the horse's rope. "Is it Dolee?"

Ben did not answer. Instead, he gently patted the horse's neck and then cautiously moved the heavy leather cow hide away. It was Dolee.

She was slumped against the horse's neck and her eyes were wide open.

She was dead.

Ben quickly covered her back up, glanced around to see if Camran was coming, and was prepared to stop him before he saw her that way. A man should see his dead wife with her eyes closed as though she merely went to sleep. It was somehow more comforting that way.

He felt Dolee move.

"She is alive!" Ben shouted. He carefully pulled her down off the horse and then lifted her into his arms. Soon the news was being shouted down the valley and more men came running including, Neil and Camran.

At first Camran was relieved, but once he saw her, he feared she had come home to die. She seemed to weigh next to nothing when he took her out of Ben's arms and started back to their cottage. He could not get her there fast enough. Never before had he realized how many steps it took to get from the pasture to the village, but even when other men offered to carry her, he simply could not let go.

At length, he carried her inside their cottage and was grateful her brother was already there building a bigger fire in the hearth. Camran gently laid Dolee down in his bed. "Dolee?" She did not answer, but she did try to open her eyes. "You are home now, love, and I will not let you die."

Camran hoped she heard him and as quickly as he could, he checked her for broken bones and injuries. Except for her cold legs, she seemed all in one piece. He wrapped her upper body back up and began to rub the circulation back into her legs. He nodded when his sister-in-law brought in some warm broth and watched her set it on the table. Then he covered Dolee's legs, pulled a chair close to the bed and reached for the spoon. He did not even notice when Neil came in.

It was then that he fully saw how gaunt Dolee's face looked and he wondered how long it had been since she had eaten. He hoped the smell would wake her more fully, so he passed the spoon full of broth under her nose.

At first, her eyes fluttered and then she opened them. Her voice was weak, but she managed to utter a few words, "I ran out of food."

"You will have plenty now." He slipped his hand behind her neck, lifted her head a little and touched the spoon to her lower lip. Camran waited until she opened her mouth and then fed her the warm liquid. Again and again, he filled her mouth, but it did not take long for her to run out of enough energy to eat, so he let her lay her head back down and sleep.

Camran could not take his eyes off her and his heart overflowed with the love he feared he would never feel again. His sweet Dolee was finally home.

*

Two days later, while she was still trying to regain her strength, the story of how Dolee managed to survive alone for so long was on everyone's lips.

"I could never do that," Nessa groaned.

Ros took her hand and walked with her down the path toward the river. "You would if you had to. Thank goodness she took her bow and arrows or she would not have had even an occasional squirrel to eat."

"Did she get lost the day she left or the next day when it was cloudy?"

Ros frowned. "I neglected to find out which day. The important thing is she found a deserted cottage in the forest with enough dry wood to keep her warm."

"But if she was lost, how did she find us?"

He stopped and wrapped both arms around Nessa. "It was her last hope. She thought she was about to die and hoped the horses would take her home. How she managed to mount the horse at all is beyond me."

"How long did it take her to get home?"

Ros smiled. "Less than a day. She must have been going in circles before she found that cottage."

"Less than a day, and all those nights lost and alone? How very dreadful. But why did she do it? She surely knew she has no sense of direction."

He quickly kissed his betrothed on the lips and then held her close. "That reminds me, you must not fear I will set you aside for any reason, do you hear me Nessa?"

She pulled back and looked into his eyes. "What are you saying that for?"

"There is an edict in our land that if a woman does not bear a child in the first three years, her husband may set her aside and take another. I want you to know that will never happen to us."

Nessa fiddled with the edge of the piece of plaid he wore over his shoulder and grinned. "We sisters have an edict of our own. If a husband sets one of us aside, he best not live in the same village as we do."

She enjoyed his laughter. After the weeks of worry and upset over Dolee, Nessa found she enjoyed the laughter of everyone in the clan a lot more. At last the world was set right again.

*

As soon as he sat down on the bed beside her and took her in his arms Dolee rested her head against her husband's shoulder. She was still exhausted, still needed to eat more to regain her strength and still worried that Camran would never forgive her. But there was a new light in his eyes -- a light she needlessly risked her life to see.

Every morning for the past two weeks, she had thrown up and this time it did not look as though it was going to go away.

-end-

CATLIN

CHAPTER I

Spring brought a renewal of life to the MacGreagor Clan, just as it always did. The sheep were sheared, the wool washed and then dyed. From there it went to the spinners who expertly wove the yarn, wrapped it in balls and took it to the weavers. Delighted with having something to do once more, the weavers set their looms back up and began to work.

The hunters hunted, the tanners tanned and the cobbler, and the men with strong hands began again to sew warm coats and make shoes. Candle makers gathered beeswax, farmers began to sow their fields and Ben made wagers with Alison on which mare would foal first. The cattle were moved to greener pastures and the builders renewed their work on the new cottages. That meant the cabinetmakers went back to making more furniture, more wood was chopped and more shavings were gathered and stored for use as kindling in the hearths.

The men also went back to practicing their warrior skills and rebuilding whatever strength was lost to them over the winter. The sisters again delighted them all with their songs at the end of each day, and a new baby seemed to be born nearly every night.

The English brides-to-be gathered in the courtyard every morning, weather permitting, where Jessup, Bethia and Greer taught them Gaelic. The afternoons were filled with washing, bathing, the baking of bread, and excitement for the coming evening when the men would come to take them for a ride or a walk.

The children, who were bad, tended the chores Neil handed out as punishment and the ones who had been good, or were not yet caught, pretended to be brave warriors or Scottish queens.

But for everyone, two things never changed in the land of the MacGreagors -- falling in love and spreading gossip.

*

It was the most unexpected sight they could have imagined. Late in the afternoon, the usual whistles announced the arrival of two women and one man. That the women were escorted by only one man was usual enough, but what the strangers wore was something the MacGreagors never thought they would see again -- Cameron plaids.

There was a time when the Camerons and the MacGreagors were close friends, fighting wars side by side and intermarrying, but much had happened since then. The Camerons refused to help when the MacDonalds attacked and the MacGreagors had not forgotten.

However, to see Camerons here sharpened Neil's curiosity. He sent four men to escort them up the glen and soon they were in the courtyard where he and Glenna were waiting. Neil searched their faces, but he did not recognize any of them.

When the man began to dismount, Neil nodded and two MacGreagor men went to help the women down. Then the three strangers stood wordlessly before the laird of the MacGreagor Clan. They were all three young and seemed to be in good condition. In unison, the women curtsied and the man bowed.

"I am Neil MacGreagor, who might you be?"

The man wrinkled his brow. "But you do not wear MacGreagor colors."

"It is a long story."

"I am Thomas and this is my sister Julia. We are the only remaining children of Rachel and Connor Cameron."

Neil's eyes instantly brightened. "Then you are my cousins."

"Finally we have found you," Julia breathed. When Neil opened his arms, she gladly went into them.

Neil released her and locked forearms with Thomas, "You are more than welcome here."

Julia looked more like her father than her mother with blond hair and blue eyes. She was taller than the other woman and she looked exhausted. "It has taken us two very long months to find you."

Glenna quickly went to her. "I am Neil's wife and I have just the thing. We managed to bring a bathing basin with us and a warm bath will comfort you."

Julia grinned first at Glenna and then at Neil. "A heated bath? I cannot wait."

Neil suspected he already knew, but he had to ask. "Have my aunt and uncle passed?"

As large in stature as any MacGreagor with his mother's dark hair and bright blue eyes, Thomas nodded. "We lost them and two brothers in the plague."

It was harder to hear than he expected and Neil bowed his head for a moment. Then his smile returned, but when he looked, the second woman was not smiling. "Who might the other lass be?"

"She is Catlin Cameron. It was her idea to come to you and until today I believed her daft. But we have found you after all."

Any other time, Neil would have opened his arms even to a stranger, but something in Catlin's eyes warned him not to, so he simply nodded. "You are welcome also. My wife adores indulging newcomers. You will have clean clothing, soft beds and more than enough to eat."

Glenna led the way inside and Julia and Thomas followed, but Catlin did not. Instead, she stared at Neil. "I would speak to you alone."

He nodded and then indicated the path they would take with his outstretched hand. He walked beside the strange woman of few words and no smile, found a deserted place near the river and encouraged her to sit on a large rock. Then he spread his legs, locked his hands behind his back and waited.

She seemed to struggle with the words and glanced at Neil twice before she decided to continue. He was such a large man, something her mother failed to mention. But he looked kind so perhaps she could trust him. Besides, she really had no other choice. "My mother said if ever I heard a certain name, I should go to you and ask for sanctuary."

"What name?"

"Charlet."

Both his eyebrows shot up. "You are Bridget's daughter?"

She let out a relieved breath. "Aye, how did you know that?"

He was confused by her question and carefully examined her eyes to see if the lass was playing some sort of game. Her hair was not the flaming red of her mother's but the sunlight brought out a considerable amount of it in her auburn curls. However her eyes were the same green as her mother's and she was as small as he remembered Bridget to be. "You do not know who Charlet is?"

"Nay, I know only that the king of England has put a bounty on her head. Do you know where she is?"

"And that is all your mother told you?"

"She said you could explain it. Can you?"

"First, tell me what has happened to your parents."

"Father and my brothers died in the plague. Mother died trying to give birth and the babe died with her. I have no one left."

Neil again lowered his eyes to take in the loss of Bridget and Blair, and then he tried to reassure their daughter. "You have all of us left. Your father was once friend to my father and your mother was once a MacGreagor." He sat down on the rock beside her and folded his arms. "So many were lost, but I suspected Blair was not alive or he would have yet been laird over the Camerons. I am grieved to hear about your mother."

Catlin was too tired for pleasantries and not at all interested in discussing the deaths of her parents. "Who is Charlet?"

"It is a very long story. We should probably see to your rest first."

"Laird MacGreagor, I..."

"Neil."

"Neil, I have come a very long way to hear the answer. Please do not keep me waiting."

He again studied the sincerity in her eyes. "Very well, Charlet was your mother."

Catlin's face jutted forward and her mouth fell open.

CHAPTER II

He let Catlin absorb his words for a moment before he continued. "Your mother took the name Bridget so the English could not find her."

"But why?"

"Because she was once in line to inherit the throne."

Catlin's eyes grew even wider. "Of England?"

"Aye." He watched her put her head in her hands and felt sorry for having shocked her. "We too have heard the English are looking for her and wondered where she was. At least now they will not find her."

She slowly raised her head and looked at him. "They meant to kill her if they did, am I right?"

"I believe so. Some in England want your mother to take the throne, but the new king is a jealous lad." Neil hesitated, but it had to be said. "Catlin, you must not tell anyone."

She took a deep breath and slowly let it out. "I am in danger."

"Aye. You are the only remaining child and you inherited her claim to the throne." His words left her speechless and he could just imagine the thoughts racing through her mind. "You are tired and we have plenty of time to talk. For now, we need to get you out of that Cameron plaid and find the best way to keep you safe. From this day forward, you belong to your mother's people. You are a MacGreagor and we are proud to claim you."

Neil helped her stand up and had she indicated a need, he would have held her and comforted her, but once more he felt Catlin put up some sort of barrier between them. When she was ready, he walked her back to the Keep and then sent her upstairs to Glenna's warm bath.

*

Upstairs, Julia and Catlin wanted to know everything that had happened since the war with the MacDonalds, of which they knew relatively little, and Glenna hardly knew where to begin. Then as soon as she began, she could not stop. She told of their escape tunnel, their journey to the new land and what they found when they got there.

As soon as Julia was bathed and dressed in new MacGreagor plaids with white shirts and a patch of cloth over her shoulder, Glenna called for the men to change the bath water. Then she sat Julia down and began to dry her hair. As they always did, the men carrying water gawked at the two new women and Glenna watched Julia's face. Julia was going to be fun to watch and one thing was clear -- the man who thought to marry Neil's cousin was in for a rougher time than he knew.

Then she noticed the look on Catlin's face. Catlin appeared not to notice the men at all and stiffly held perfectly still -- almost as though she feared one of them might try to touch her. Glenna dismissed it as shyness that would be overcome with time. Once the men were gone Catlin relaxed and while she bathed, Glenna went back to brushing Julia's hair dry and continued with her stories.

*

Neil was alone in the Great Hall when Thomas came back from

bathing in the loch and changing into a MacGreagor kilt. He dropped the meager sacks the three of them brought with them near a wall, went to enjoy the warmth of the crackling fire for a moment and grinned. "I have much to tell you, cousin."

"And I you, but first tell me about Laird Cameron. After the plague, we heard little of your people."

Thomas joined Neil at the table and accepted the goblet of wine he handed him. "The Cameron is a ruthless lad. He seized control an hour after Blair died and there were nearly fifty willing to side with him. The rest had not the strength or the desire to fight. Now they regret it, but there is little they can do. He is strong in numbers, giving over unthinkable generosity to keep his lads loyal."

"Why did the Camerons stop speaking to us?"

Thomas shrugged. "Who understands the mind of a daft lad? Laird Cameron spoke an edict not to talk to any of the other clans and we were afraid to betray him. We planned to ask for your help in our fight against him but the MacDonalds attacked you before we could."

"Who is we?"

Thomas paused to take a gulp of wine and let the warmth fill his body. "We numbered only six and twenty, mostly under the age of fifteen when we began to plan. The best of us were far more brave in speech than in actions, I must confess. The plague took seven of us, the months passed, we got older and as I said, we waited too long."

"I see. How old are you now?"

"Seventeen." Thomas downed the rest of his wine and wiped his mouth with his sleeve. "Speaking of plagues, I hasten to give you Julia."

It made Neil grin, "That bad, is she?"

"When she is riled, which is often, she breathes fire."

"And Catlin, does she breathe fire?"

"Nay, she does not take after her mother. Now there was a woman who could give you a glimpse into hell and then make you wish you were there. I swear by all that is holy I have never again taken a sweet bread without asking."

Neil laughed and was beginning to like this man very much. He reminded him a great deal of Connor. "I missed your parents after they went to live with the Camerons. I confess I did not truly understand their decision." His mind wandered back to the day Sween threw Rachel, Connor and their small children off MacGreagor land. He would never forget watching them ride up the hill and disappear over the top.

"Cousin?"

"Do forgive me, what?"

"It was my mother who tried to kill Sween."

Neil was stunned. "Aunt Rachel did it? She missed and I thought her a better shot than that." He could not help but chuckle. "You cannot know how much I regretted that missed shot. But I suppose your parents told you about all that."

"Every detail. Father often liked to tell how you outwitted your brother's lads. The older Father got, the more he liked to tell it."

"That war seems like a life time ago." Neil pushed the memories out of his mind and poured more wine into Thomas' goblet. "We are not without our worries, but we are happy here. There is some measure of relief in living without a wall in which our enemies can trap us."

"I suppose so. Tell me, when do you think the lasses will come down?"

Neil smiled. "I am laird over all but that lass upstairs, whom I call wife. She will bring them down, but in her own good time."

"It is just that we have not eaten in three days. I fear Julia and Catlin will …"

"Of course." Neil left the table and started up the stairs just as the women and little Justin were coming down. He smiled, took baby Ceanna out of Glenna's arms and kissed his wife's cheek. Then he took his son's hand. "Our guests have not eaten in three days."

"Julia just told me." Glenna opened the door, nodded to one of the servers and soon two women carried bowls filled with meat and vegetables to the table while another began to fill goblets with wine. "Come sit down," she told her guests. Glenna seated herself, waited for the others to sit down and then smiled at her husband. "A family at last." Her smile was returned by all the others and she was delighted. "I was just telling Julia and Catlin all that has happened since…"

Abruptly, the door opened and Walrick burst in. Behind him came a man with an injured, bleeding arm. "Vallam is hurt and I cannot find Gelson to sew him up."

CHAPTER III

Catlin could not believe her eyes and the injured man looked just as surprised to see her. He wore the same MacGreagor colors she now wore and his injury was her doing. She felt bad for hurting him and got up to take a closer look. She tried not to look into his accusing eyes but one glance confirmed her worse fear -- he was furious. The injury was serious, he had blood all over his clothing and he definitely needed her help. "I will sew him, bring him to the table."

Thomas got up, hurried to the wall where he left Catlin's sack, grabbed it and took it to her. "Catlin is the best we have at sewing skin. She is quick and it will hurt less that way."

If there was hesitation on Vallam's part, no one seemed to notice and Catlin was certain she would have. She took hold of his uninjured arm, guided Vallam to the table and then took a seat across from him while Glenna grabbed extra cloths and Neil finished clearing that end of the table.

Julia was skittish when it came to the sight of blood. Ravenously hungry, she picked up her bowl and went to stand against a far wall. She took a bite, decided it would go down easier if she diverted her eyes completely and turned until her back was to the others.

Neil gave the baby back to Glenna and grabbed his goblet of wine off the table. He handed it to Vallam and went to get the flask so he could refill it. By then, Walrick was helping wipe the blood away from the wound while Catlin found her needle and thread in her sack.

He was in a lot of pain but Vallam's anger far outweighed his suffering and he was happy to have the wine both to calm him and to dull the pain. He drank and then drank again as soon as Neil refilled the goblet, yet he kept one eye on Catlin as she threaded the needle.

Finally, she looked at him and he was suddenly taken aback. She had the most remarkable green eyes he had ever seen and for a moment, he lost his ire. Then he remembered his anger and renewed his scowl.

"The wound is not as deep as I feared. Try not to move," said Catlin.

He doubted he could move with Walrick holding his wrist down, but he nodded. He prepared himself for the poke of the needle, but it was not too bad and before long she had taken two quick stitches in his forearm, wiped more blood away and started a third.

Neil watched for a time and then asked the inevitable question, "What happened?"

But Vallam kept his eyes on Catlin who seemed unwilling to look at him a second time. "I was attacked by three hundred lads and narrowly escaped with my life."

Neil exchanged knowing glances with Walrick and when Justin pulled on his kilt, he lifted the boy up so he could watch. For generations when a man got hurt but found the cause embarrassing, he told the same story. He was attacked by three hundred men but managed to escape. "And you did not recognize the clan's colors?"

Again, Catlin concentrated on her sewing and again Vallam watched her reaction. "I had not seen those colors before." Her face was as stoic as any man's and although he was still furious with her, he admired her lack of emotion.

"Have you any other injuries?" Catlin asked.

If anyone had been paying close attention, they might have noticed a slight flicker of rage in his eyes. Now she was toying with him. She knew good and well he had another injury and she knew exactly where. He decided to do a little toying of his own. "I do."

"Do you require more stitches?"

"I cannot be sure."

She hesitated, but this man was different from any other she had known. His mind was sharp and he understood what she was doing. Catlin fully expected him to tell Neil the truth and when he did not, her good opinion of him increased. Now she wondered just how far she could go before he lost his temper. To her, it was an important thing to know. "And why is that?"

"The injury is beneath my kilt and I have not looked. Perhaps you..." Suddenly Glenna had her hand on his shoulder. Vallam quickly glanced up to see who it was, realized he forgot there were other women in the room, and glanced at Neil to see how much trouble he was in. But both Neil and Walrick were fascinated with the way Catlin was crisscrossing the stitches in his arm.

Neil watched her take three more stitches and then expertly tie off the thread without getting a drop of blood on her own clothing. "Well done, where did you learned to do that?"

"My father taught me." She carefully put away her needle and thread. "The bleeding should stop now." She reviewed her work for a second more, put her needle and thread away, stood up and went to the wash bowl. As soon as her hands were clean and dry she retook her place at the table and began to eat. "I am starved."

Her demeanor implied she had not been affected at all by seeing an injured man and Thomas enjoyed the look of surprise on the faces of the others. "Catlin may look like an angel, but she has a heart as hard as rock and I should know, I have tried to soften it often enough." He winked at Glenna and went to put Catlin's sack back where he found it.

Catlin shrugged and hurried to swallow her bite of food. "I cannot tell you how happy I was when Thomas gave up…at last."

Thomas ignored her remark, sat down next to her and grinned at Neil. "She is just a tiny bit useful or else we would not have brought her with us."

"I am pleased you did. Not many of us can manage the sewing of flesh." Neil walked to the far wall and touched Julia's elbow. "You can look now."

She rolled her eyes and followed him back to the table just in time to spot the bloody cloths Walrick was carrying out. Quickly, she turned her eyes away.

Vallam waited, but still Catlin would not look at him. "I thank you for sewing me," he managed to mumble. He did not mean a word of it but he knew Neil expected him to say something. Without waiting for her nod, he turned and followed Walrick out.

With all of them finally back in their places and the baby content to be on her back on the table playing with her toes, they ate in silence for a while before Neil directed his question to Thomas. "Tell me more about Laird Cameron."

Thomas quickly took a sip of wine to wash down his food. "There are words to describe a lad like that, but I dare not say them in front of the lasses. He is…"

"Stupid," Julia interrupted. "He ordered new shoes, did not approve of the sewing and killed the cobbler. 'Twas the only cobbler we had!"

Glenna nearly spilled her wine when she started to laugh.

Julia continued, "Laird Cameron suffers terrible nightmares, convinced the MacGreagor ghost is coming to kill him. He heard about the one that did in The Ferguson and he has not had a peaceful night since."

"Nor have we," Catlin muttered.

"She is right," admitted Julia. "He drinks so he can sleep, then he is belligerent, loud and unthinkably cruel. It was all we lasses could do to stay clear of him."

Neil pushed his bowl away. "Then I am even more pleased you have come to us."

"Is it true the MacGreagor will kill any lad who hurts a lass?" Catlin asked.

"Aye, it is true."

Glenna checked to see that Justin was eating and then curled her little finger so the baby could chew on her knuckle. "Our lads are too strong and it does not take much for a lad to hurt a lass or a child. It is an old family edict and I highly approve. I would that more clans had the edict."

An odd silence followed and Neil wondered if there was something they were not telling, but he dismissed the thought. "Did you happen to go to the MacGreagor hold before you came?"

"Have you not heard it is haunted?" Seated between his sister and Catlin, Thomas mischievously grinned, took another bite and then pushed his bowl away. "However, I did lay flowers on the graves of your parents. It was my mother's final wish."

Julia glared at her brother. "That was not her final wish. Her dying wish was for you to marry; though she did not hold out much hope any lass would have you."

"That is strange, she told me to marry you off as quickly as I could and to use bribery if need be."

Catlin rolled her eyes. "They carry on this way incessantly. The poor lass must have lingered for weeks before she got all her final wishes said."

"Nay," argued Thomas, "She simply spoke very quickly. And just now I am reminded. Do the MacGreagors have a cobbler? I was learning that trade when our cobbler met his untimely demise."

Julia again glared at her brother. "Because you tied the threads on the inside of Laird Cameron's shoes, instead of the outside where they would not hurt."

"Sister, are you implying I am somehow at fault?"

"Nay, I am boldly accusing you of intentionally trying to raise the Cameron's ire."

Thomas puffed his cheeks and noticed everyone was waiting for his answer. "Very well then, I am caught. But how was I to know Laird Cameron would kill our only cobber over such a trifling thing?"

For another hour they talked and laughed. But as the women grew wearier, Glenna reminded her husband they needed rest and then she took all three of their guests to the beds the servers had prepared in two of the cottages.

When she came back, Neil and Walrick were talking and to her surprise, Neil was not smiling. As soon as she took her seat at the table, Neil covered her hand with his. "Catlin is Charlet's daughter."

Glenna slowly closed her eyes. "Does she understand how much danger she is in?"

"She does now. Before today, she did not know her mother was Charlet. Her parents are dead and there are no other children."

Glenna helped herself to more wine. "We should spread the word that Charlet is dead so the English will stop looking for her."

"Aye, but how do we do it without the rumor leading back to us?"

CHAPTER IV

The little cottage Glenna took Catlin and Julia to was clean and held a bowl of fresh flowers floating in water on the table, a clan tradition of sorts. Julia was so tired she quickly collapsed into the nearest bed and went right to sleep.

Catlin spread a plaid over her and then walked to the other bed. Next to it, a candle on a small table gave off the sweet smell of honey. She turned down the covers, unbuckled her belt and caught her MacGreagor plaid before it fell to the floor. Carefully, she folded it, laid it and her belt across the back of a chair and climbed into bed wearing only her long shirt.

She scooted down, covered herself and rested her head on her arm, but as exhausted as she was, her eyes remained wide open - Catlin Cameron MacGreagor was in line to inherit the throne of England. It was a thought she could not manage to fully grasp.

*

The next morning, Neil took Thomas to see the cobbler and then took Julia to meet some of the young women her age. Once they were distracted, he asked Catlin to walk with him and soon they were joined by Glenna and Walrick.

Neil found a clean area, spread the plaid he brought with him on the grass and helped Glenna sit while Walrick helped Catlin. Then the men crossed their feet at the ankle and sat down. Their usual guards were there but too far away to hear.

Neil pulled a blade of grass out of the meadow and examined it. "Catlin, Walrick is my second and he remembers your mother. He is here to help you. Glenna is my wife from whom I have no secrets.

"I see." She looked at Glenna, at Walrick and then at Neil, "When I was growing up, there were rumors that Bridget was not my mother's true name, but I believed none of it and never was the name 'Charlet' mentioned. How could my mother be English? She said Scotland was the only home she had ever known."

"Your mother was but a few days old when the king asked my father to hide her. Father let the clan believe she had been abandoned, gave her the name Charlet and she happily grew up among the MacGreagors. Then one day, the cottage she shared with the man and lass who cared for her caught fire. They died and she survived. Not long after, father got word an Englishman wanted her hand in marriage."

"Did she know this Englishman?" Catlin asked.

"She had never laid eyes on any Englishman and my father grew immediately suspicious. To keep her safe, he asked Blair Cameron to hide her. At the time, your mother knew nothing more than my father did - she was English not Scottish and she was in danger. By the time it was safe enough for her to come home, mother had spoken to the king, learned Charlet was his niece and first in line to inherit the crown. It was the king's nephew who tried to kill her, for which he was executed."

"But she did not become queen."

"Nay, by then your mother loved your father too much to leave him."

Catlin's mouth dropped. "She turned down the throne of England?"

Neil was surprised by her reaction. "Have you any doubt she loved your father that much?"

"I could never love a lad *that* much."

Glenna smiled and patted Catlin's hand. "I said the same at your age. But when..."

Catlin ignored her. "Is the present king in line before or behind my mother?"

Still caught off guard, Neil tried to read what Catlin was thinking. Slowly, he answered, "I dare say he is behind or he would not be looking for her."

"And the English want her to be queen?"

"Some do."

Catlin was becoming angry and she did not know exactly why. To stall for time, she ran her fingers through the sides of her long auburn hair. "And now that she is dead, am I before or after this new king in lineage?"

"I do not know." A thousand thoughts were running through Neil's mind. A Scot becoming the Queen of England opened a lot of good possibilities. Catlin hiding among the MacGreagor Clan opened a lot of dangerous possibilities too. "There might be a way to find out, if it becomes important."

"It is important to me."

"Why?"

Catlin was not ready to speak her thoughts and decided instead to dismiss the subject. "You are right, Laird MacGreagor. It does not really matter."

Neil was not fooled. "I am concerned you do not clearly see the danger. Without careful thought you could bring the whole of England down upon us."

Catlin got to her knees, accepted Walrick's help and stood up. "I am not as simple minded as you assume." With that...and without anyone's permission, she turned and walked away.

Glenna started to call after her but Neil grabbed her hand. "Let her go."

*

Cured of the incessant stomachaches he had as a newborn, Jessup's son was sleeping peacefully when Glenna, Neil and Walrick came to visit. She invited them to sit down and then offered each a goblet of water or wine. The men declined and remained standing, but Glenna accepted a chair and the wine.

"Have you ever heard the name, Charlet?" Neil asked.

Jessup's eyes lit up. "Ah, you have come to talk of ghosts and fables. I am enthralled."

"Then you have heard of her?"

"In a manner of speaking. She is illusive and the last I heard only a few have ever seen her. She has red hair, or so they report, and she was once first in line to the throne. But she disappeared and I think someone did her in years ago."

"Why do you think that?"

"Because she never again was seen. My beloved king Richard asked that she be found after he took the throne, but nothing ever came of it … at least not that he told me. I dearly wish we did know where she is. Charlet is possibly our only hope of getting the throne out of the hands of the wretched George of Leics."

"What if Charlet died, but had a child before she passed. What say you about that?" Neil asked.

Jessup slowly turned to look into Neil's eyes. "Which one?"

"Which one what?"

"Which of the three Camerons is Charlet's child? Wait; if Thomas and Julia are your cousins, then it must be Catlin. Of course it is Catlin; I should have guessed by the way she holds herself." Jessup could hardly contain her excitement, stood up and clapped her hands. "She is royalty, Neil. She belongs to England and England needs her."

"Jessup, do you not see the complications? We are Scots and we cannot march into England even if Scotland might be the better for it."

"Of course not. On the other hand, once they get wind that she is here we will have the English marching up our glen wanting to kill her."

"They will not get wind of it."

"Not as long as they think Charlet is still alive. Once they know she is not, they will search for her children."

Neil hung his head. "I had not thought of that."

The whole time, Walrick stood with his hands behind his back listening. "Perhaps we could start a rumor that Charlet boarded a ship bound for France several years ago."

Jessup smiled. "I doubt George has neglected to look for her there already. Nay, you best not start any rumors at all. Let the other clans think you have no interest in the subject." She turned her attention back to Neil. "Does Catlin know?"

"She does now and I was not pleased with her reaction. I believe her thinking matches yours on the subject, although she sees it in a different light than that of freeing her countrymen from an unrighteous king."

Glenna rolled her eyes, "You mean she covets the crown for her own gain? You cannot know that."

"I do not care in what light she sees it," Jessup said, retaking her seat. "George of Leics is a liar and a murderer. I will be more than pleased if Catlin can manage to dethrone him no matter her intentions."

Glenna reached across the table and took hold of her friend's hand. "Before we decide her future we should get to know her better. Perhaps she wants to be queen, and perhaps she wants no part of the English."

"She is right," said Walrick. 'What daughter of Scotland would want to be English? It is unthinkable."

CHAPTER V

She wanted to mount her horse, race away and feel the wind in her hair. But she had no idea where her horse was. Instead, Catlin continued to walk down the glen. At first, she walked quickly to release her anger. Her thoughts were in turmoil and her questions had no easy answers.

It appeared to be true her mother was English and set to inherit the throne. It was also true Charlet declined so she could marry Catlin's father. Catlin still could not see how any man could be that important, but alas, that was her mother's decision.

She realized the truth greatly enlightened her as to her upbringing. Often she thought her parents ridiculously overprotective and was angry when they prohibited certain events. Now she was sorry for her anger and wished she could take back some of the words she said. It was useless to dwell on that too and she quickly set it aside.

Catlin took a deep breath, slowed her pace, and tried again to assess the situation. Did she or did she not want to claim the throne of England? The question was too monumental and she regretted with all her heart that her mother was not there to answer her questions. She regretted it so much she was about to cry.

Suddenly, she realized a man was walking behind her and she caught her breath. She stopped and quickly turned around. It was only the man she cut...who, no doubt, was expecting an apology. His timing could not be worse and she had no desire to deal with him at the moment, so she glared hoping he would go away. "I prefer to walk alone."

Vallam rolled his eyes. "I prefer to let you but our laird disagrees. MacGreagor women are not allowed to leave the village alone."

"I am not..." she started to say she was not a MacGreagor, but realized that was no longer true. "I am not leaving the village."

"Unfortunately for me."

Her glare grew hotter and for a moment, she forgot her intention not to deal with him just now. She was about to chastise him when she abruptly changed her mind. She might as well get this over with. "I am sorry I hurt you."

"You do not look sorry nor did you look sorry yesterday. In fact, you look quite pleased with yourself."

Frustrated, Catlin turned her back to him and walked away. "You are refusing to accept my apology? Very well then."

Vallam was no more interested in discussing the situation than she was, but Neil saw him watching Catlin head down the glen and nodded for him to guard her. He would rather be doing a thousand other things and he was hardly fit to protect her with his arm hurt, but until someone came to relieve him, he was stuck. As he had been for what seemed hours, he continued to follow her.

Vallam spent half the night thinking about her green eyes and wondering if he was mad at her for hurting him or mad at himself for letting her. The truth be told, he did not even hear her approach and it was not until she reached through the bush and tried to steal the bird he just finished cleaning, that he realized she was there. Had it been a man's hand, he might have reacted differently, but the delicate long fingers were definitely those of a woman and in the blink of an eye, he grabbed her hand. Just as quickly, she cut him. He grabbed her other hand, pulled her out of the bush and should have suspected what she might do next, but she was far too quick and before he could stand back she shoved her knee hard into his groin. The pain was excruciating and he had no choice but to let go and double over.

That he let a woman hurt him was unbearably humiliating and he waited until dark hoping not to have to explain. He intended to slip into his cottage and forgo the stitching, but Walrick spotted the blood and insisted. What a shock to find Catlin a guest at the table of his laird. "Thank you."

Catlin stopped and turned to stare at him. "For what?"

"For not telling Neil I let you get the better of me."

"I am many things, but I do not delight in making others appear witless. Now if you will please not interrupt me further, I have a great deal to think about."

Her attitude was unpleasant, her glare irritating, her manners inexcusable and he could not help but return her foul expression. He slightly nodded and silently vowed never to speak to her again. A few minutes later she again turned around, but this time it was not to talk to him. She passed by without so much as a glance, headed back toward the village and did not let him see those fascinating green eyes.

Catlin was not even thinking about the man following her. What she desperately wanted – what she actually came here for was help with an altogether different problem. The throne of England offered her a magnificent way to exact the revenge she sought, but then what? She did not want to be the Queen of England, not really. In fact, just like her mother she had never even seen an Englishman. If Neil refused to help with her other problem, she would be better off going to Scotland's king.

Her head was starting to hurt and when she noticed Julia hurrying toward her, she welcomed the diversion.

By the time she arrived, Julia was nearly out of breath. "Did you ask Neil? Has he agreed to help us?"

Catlin glanced back at Vallam and lowered her voice. "You must not speak so loudly."

Julia paused a moment to calm her breathing. "I saw you talking to Neil and thought…"

"Nay, I did not ask him."

"Oh. I suppose it is too soon, but I do so want to see the look on Lammond's face when we kill him."

"So do I, but Thomas is right. We must give the MacGreagors time to know and trust us before we ask. Come, there is a chill in the air and we must go inside." She glanced back just in time to see Vallam holding his forearm and felt a twinge of regret. She turned, walked to him and smiled, which seemed to lessen his scowl a bit. "May I see the wound?"

Her sudden change in attitude confused him and he did not trust her. "Why?"

"I wish to see if the stitches held well enough."

He reluctantly nodded. She tried to push his sleeve up, but the cloth caught on the stitches so he let down the strip of cloth over his shoulder and took that side of his shirt off. Then he glanced at Julia's refusal to look and was amused. "It is not bleeding."

Julia slightly glanced at him and then looked away not wanting to even see a wound, let alone any blood. "Pray do not tell any of your friends what a wretched mother I will be. Finding a suitable husband is difficult enough as it is." But the lad didn't seem to hear her.

Catlin's reaction to Vallam's muscular upper body surprised her. It excited her and made her furious all at the same time. His body was the last thing she wanted to think about just now. She had not noticed before, but he was a fairly handsome man. His blond hair was naturally wavy, his eyes, which she only slightly looked at, were a dusty blue and his face was square.

Determined to hide her reaction, she forced herself to quickly examine the wound, take a step back and divert her eyes. "Julia is only without a husband, because she rejects all that are brave enough to ask." She turned, looped her arm through Julia's, and started toward the village again. "I am still hungry, if you can believe it. I fear I shall never be full."

He watched her walk away, put his shirt back on and tucked it in his belt. Her touch on his arm was soft, he found it oddly pleasing and noticed she seemed unwilling to look him in the eye when she finished. He wanted just one up close look at her eyes in the sunlight, but she denied him and he reminded himself he didn't care...but he did care and with that truth he was unhappy.

*

Neil did not have to guess how Thomas and the cobbler were getting along, the cobbler was beside himself with laughter when Neil knocked and then went inside. A few minutes later, he and Thomas walked out and headed up the path toward the Keep. "Have you been a distraction all day?"

"Not *all* day, perhaps."

"Most of the day?"

"Not *most* of the day, perhaps."

Neil rolled his eyes. "At least your stories cannot last forever. There are many MacGreagors who need shoes."

"Fortunately, I have mastered the practice of telling stories and working at the same time."

"It is not you that concerns me. Is the cobbler able to do the same?"

"I quite see your meaning, cousin."

"Good."

"Do you plan to fetch me every day?"

Neil stopped and looked at him. "Do you require it? I was under the impression you were old enough to manage on your own."

"You do so remind me of my mother. I could never get away with a thing around her either." A slow grin crossed Thomas' face. "You heard I was getting out of hand, came to trample me to the ground and see that I do not do it again."

"I came to ask you a question." Neil continued down the path and looked away so the lad could not see his smile.

"Oh." Thomas hurried to catch up. "What question?"

"My wife and I enjoy matchmaking. What sort of lad would make a good husband for Catlin?"

"Nothing short of a wild boar would do. I have offered to take on the dreaded responsibility myself, but she does not see the advantages of being married to me, a lad without a home, a trade and only one irritating sister for a family."

Again Neil stopped to read Thomas' face. "Do you love her?"

"I believe I first fell in love with her when I was five. She socked me in the eye and from then on I have been hopelessly smitten." He studied Neil's frown and decided his cousin was serious. "Oh, you mean do I love her more than any other? Nay, I love all women the same. It is a curse."

"And Julia, what kind of husband do you believe she will need?" Neil asked as they started to walk again.

"I take it back; keep the wild boar for Julia." He was hardly paying attention when they entered the great hall where Catlin, Julia and Glenna were talking.

To the amazement of both Neil and Glenna, Julia ran to her brother, threw her arms around him and planted a kiss on his cheek. "I missed you so."

Shocked, Thomas instantly took hold of her arms and held her away from him. "Now you've done it, they will think we love each other."

"Is that a blush I see, brother?" Her eyes danced with delight. "Finally, I have gotten the better of you first."

He moved away, wiped her kiss off his cheek with the back of his hand, straightened his kilt and looked at Neil. "I begged mother for another brother, but she gave me *Julia*."

Julia looked at Neil also and began to pout. "Mother said you would make me a different village to live in. When may I have my own village? I do not believe I am able to suffer this brother very much longer."

"My dear sister, you remind me of why I have not yet taken a wife."

"And you somehow think you have a say in the matter? Anyone can see why no lass will have you."

*

For the second time in two days, Neil and Glenna were pleased with the company of the newest members of the clan for the evening meal. Neil maintained his place at the head of the table while Glenna sat across from the three, drank in every word they said and watched Catlin repeatedly roll her eyes when Thomas and Julia bantered about.

As soon as one told a story of their childhood, the other bettered it by telling another story. Before long, they seemed to run out of stories and the subject turned to Catlin, whom they were happy to say, might as well have been a sister, for one never went far without the other two.

Thomas sat up straight and squared his shoulders. "I promised Blair I would love and defend his daughter and that is precisely what I intend to do."

Glenna quickly looked at Catlin and was surprised by her lack of any reaction at all.

When she realized everyone was waiting, Catlin leaned around Julia to look Thomas in the eye. "My father was ill when we made our pledge and we only did it to help him rest. I am grateful for your protection, but you need not marry me."

Thomas shrugged. "Marriage … protection, I fail to see the difference."

"Of course you do," Julia scoffed. "You are…"

"You took a pledge?" Neil asked.

Both Thomas and Catlin looked at him, but it was Thomas who answered. "Aye, but neither of us meant it. We only…"

"Actually, the pledge saved my life." Catlin interrupted.

Julia reached out and took Catlin's hand, "You do not have to tell them."

"I know." Catlin lowered her eyes for a moment before she continued. "There is a particular Cameron who pestered me to marry him and did not let me be until I told him I was pledged to Thomas."

Thomas put on a smug expression. "I was far bigger and much better trained, I am proud to say…"

This time it was Julia who rolled her eyes. "Never mind the scar on his backside that prevented him from sitting for nearly a month."

"Sister, you are well aware I could not retrieve my sword without bending over. It could happen to anyone."

Neil laughed. "Thomas, are you in need of training?"

In unison, Thomas said, "Nay," and Julia said, "Aye."

Neil laughed again and then finished his meal, pushed his bowl away and listened to them tell another two stories they had forgotten. Occasionally he glanced at Catlin who was again quiet although not in the least forlorn or upset. Still he could not help but think there was something more to the story of the man who wanted to marry her. Then when Thomas mentioned Laird Cameron's son, he thought he saw Catlin shiver.

It was as though Neil read her mind and she was aghast when he asked how many they were forced to leave behind. Thomas and Julia immediately got quiet and waited for Catlin to answer, "Too many."

Jessup was right, Neil thought, there was something regal about Catlin. He noticed she always sat up straight and when he began to talk to her, she set her spoon down and put her hands in her lap. "What do you wish to tell me?"

Catlin did not flinch. "We came to beg your assistance. The women are shamed repeatedly and the men who object are executed. You are our only hope."

"Have you been shamed?"

Glenna gasped. "Neil, she is unmarried and…"

Catlin reassured Glenna with her smile. "You forget I have Thomas to defend me." She calmly turned to Neil again. "Will you help us?"

Neil stared into her eyes. "Are you asking us to go to war?"

CHAPTER VI

Thomas rose out of his chair, walked to the hearth, grabbed a stick and used it to stir the embers. "We have no right to ask you to risk your lives, but there must be a way to stop the madness. Friends…good friends have died trying to protect sisters or wives and perhaps I should have…"

"Nay!" Julia got up and hurried to her brother. "Mother was right, you are more use to us alive than dead. You got us here and without you, God only knows what might have become of the two of us."

Thomas hugged his sister with genuine affection. "I would go daft if anything happened to you."

"Is it that dreadful?" Glenna asked.

Catlin answered, "Lammond Cameron seeks to bed any women he can and puts lads in cages for sport. His father is laird and we are nothing more to either of them than entertainment."

"Cages?" Neil whispered.

Thomas lowered his eyes. "They are too short for a lad my size and I do not possess enough words to say of the pain."

"He put you in a cage like an animal?"

Julia walked back to the table and sat down beside Glenna. "Do not hate us; we have to ask for help."

Glenna put a loving hand to Julia's cheek. "I could never hate you."

"I have a suggestion," Catlin said. "Threaten to make the father's nightmares of the MacGreagor ghost come true."

Glenna grinned, "Frighten him to death?"

Catlin emphatically nodded. "It would not take much. Spread the word that a thousand MacGreagors are coming to seek their revenge and he would most likely succumb before you even leave home."

Each of them laughed and tried to remain light hearted for the rest of the evening, but the subject was just under the surface. Neil often looked at Thomas, his own flesh and blood and tried to imagine him locked in a cage that was too short for him to stretch out. The very idea made him furious and going to war was no longer out of the question.

Neil had to know, so just before he sent them off to their rest he asked Thomas one last question. "How long did he leave you in the cage?"

Thomas lowered his gaze and did not quickly answer, "Eight days."

"And for what were you punished?"

"For not killing him when I had the chance."

*

The next morning, Catlin found the rush of the water in the river soothing and decided to walk down the bank. But when she glanced back, a man was following her. His kilt was green, the same as a Cameron kilt and the way he kept coming toward her made her wary.

Luag was confused. Neil assigned him to stay close enough to protect Catlin, but he had done nothing to frighten her. She kept looking back at him and the expression on her face oddly changed to discomfort and then to terror. She began to walk faster so he walked faster and when she started to run, he chased after her. He had to if he was to keep her safe.

Catlin was not even aware she was screaming. There was a man in front of her too, and as she got closer she recognized him and ran into Vallam's arms.

He looked at Luag and was just as confused. Luag would never hurt her, yet she was screaming, her whole body was trembling and she had both arms tightly wrapped around him with the back of his shirt clutched in her fists. "What is wrong, Catlin?"

She did not answer and a helpless Luag and Vallam stood there not knowing what to do. Then Vallam spotted Neil and Thomas coming at a dead run with other men not far behind.

Certain someone had hurt her, Neil was about to draw his sword when Thomas put his hand out. "Wait." As soon as he got close enough, Thomas stopped, paused for just a moment more, and then slowly walked to Vallam's side so he could see Catlin's face. She was still screaming and just as he expected, her tormented eyes were wide. He quickly glanced at the other men, suspected what had frightened her and spoke softly. "Catlin, it is not Lammond. Do you hear me Catlin? Lammond is not here."

At length, she closed her eyes, stopped screaming and took two urgent breaths. She did not let go of Vallam, but she did turn just enough to search the faces of the men and assure herself Lammond was not there.

Her body was still violently shaking and Thomas gave her a few more moments to calm down. "May I touch you now?" When she nodded, Thomas gently pushed the hair away from her face and then leaned over and kissed the top of her head. "We are safe here."

Again, she drew in a deep breath but she was still trembling and not yet ready to leave Vallam's embrace.

"What upset her?" Neil asked.

Thomas had pure disgust in his eyes when he answered. "Lammond likes to hunt the women."

Neil's mouth dropped. "Hunt them?"

"Aye, she is quick and he especially likes to hunt her." Thomas turned his attention to Luag. "If you talk to her, she will not be frightened of you. But you must tell her every move you intend to make. Julia is the same, although not quite so violently affected."

"Neil wants us to protect her," Luag said.

Thomas smiled and put a hand on Luag's shoulder. "I do not envy you your task. She is head-strong and not easy to protect." Then he turned back to Catlin, "We should have told Neil last night. I fear you have frightened the greatest of his warriors out of half their wits."

At last, she released her grip on Vallam and stepped back. "I do apologize. I am not yet fully rested and my mind played tricks on me." Still she did not look into Vallam's eyes and did not wait for his reply before she headed back down the river bank. This time she was the one who was humiliated and by her own actions. Of all the men she chose to go to for safety, why did it have to be that one?

Neil watched her go and then turned back to Thomas. "I have never seen a lass that frightened. What can we do to help her recover?"

"When last we were in the Cameron village, he caught her and she cut him before she got away. We could not stay, you see, and all of us fear the revenge he has taken on those we left behind. I promised Catlin I would go back and kill the sop once she and Julia were safe. It is a promise I intend to keep."

"And I will help you," said Neil.

*

It took less than an hour for every ear to hear how the Camerons came to them for sanctuary and how someone named Lammond liked to hunt the women like animals. The men were enraged and the women were heartsick. Some still had family living with the Camerons.

An hour after that, most of the men were gathered in the courtyard volunteering to tear this Lammond, whoever he was, limb from limb. But Neil was not ready to go marching off without a plan and told them to wait until one could be worked out.

Upstairs, Catlin and Glenna stood in the second floor window watching. "I did not mean to cause such a stir," Catlin whispered. She could not seem to take her eyes off of Vallam, the man whose arms she could still feel around her. "What is his name again?"

"Who?" Glenna studied her eyes to see where she was looking and then smiled. "Ah, his name is Vallam. You stitched his arm."

"Is he a good lad?"

"I believe so. Do you prefer him?"

"I do not think I am in a position to prefer anyone. Besides, I am so terrified of lads I cannot seem to relax around them. Even Neil frightens me a little and I know he would never hurt me."

"Yet you ran to Vallam," said Glenna.

"You will think me daft, but I thought he was my father." she smiled at her memory of him. "Come to think of it, you need no longer wonder, I confess I *am* quite daft."

"I can understand why. Oh look. See the lad standing next to him with a clean-shaven face? That is Luag, the lad who frightened you."

"Has he removed his beard for my sake?"

"I suspect he has. Neil asked him to protect you and you should be honored. Luag goes everywhere with Neil and is his second when they are away from the village. My husband is determined to see nothing happens to you."

"I *am* honored."

"Catlin, you must promise not to go for walks without one of the lads."

"I promise." Just then, she noticed Vallam watching her. She slightly nodded and then moved away from the window. "It is time."

Glenna followed her out the door and down the stairs. "Time for what?"

"To shed myself of the fear."

CHAPTER VII

Vallam kept watching but she did not return to the window and at length he looked away. He understood finally why she attacked him and how she learned to strike quickly and without hesitation. Her skill was remarkable and probably kept her alive. The image of her being hunted made his blood boil. For as long as he lived, he would never forget the terror in her voice, and he wanted nothing more than to hold her close and make her fear go away. He doubted there was a man in the clan who did not feel the same.

Even though Neil told them to go back to their duties, several of the men still lingered in the courtyard, discussing suggestions they would make. Mostly they were just expressing their rage, but sometimes the best battle ideas were borne out of rage.

There was some sort of commotion among the men and Vallam raised up to see what it was, but then the men began to part and he saw that Catlin was walking toward him. As she passed, she touched the men near her on the arm or the hand as if to let them know she did not fear them.

Catlin first went to Luag. She touched his face and smiled. "Grow it back. If you cut yourself trying to trim it daily, I will be forced to put stitches in your face and I assure you it will hurt." She returned his smile and then turned to Vallam. "Did I hurt your arm?"

"Nay, and if you did, I would not mind." At last, she looked him in the eye and did not quickly look away.

"I have come to try to get beyond my fear. It is childish and will only serve to keep me from a happy life." She turned back to Luag again. "Glenna tells me that when I wish to walk, I should tell you. Will that be acceptable?"

"Aye."

"Good." She curtsied and turned to go back. Then she noticed a woman coming through the men toward her who looked to be the same age as Glenna and Neil. She held a little one in her arms and her smile was genuine.

"I am Jessup. Glenna promised to bring you to meet me, but I fear she has forgotten."

"You are English?"

"I am. Do you speak the language?"

"Mother taught me some of the words, but…"

"Then perhaps you might practice with me. I can always use help with my Gaelic."

Catlin was not fooled. If this English woman sought her out, it was not to practice the language. "Would now be to your liking?"

Jessup was delighted. The girl seemed as intelligent as she was beautiful and regal. "It would indeed."

She nodded to Luag, smiled at Vallam and then started to take a walk with Jessup. When she glanced back, both men were following at a respectable distance. She had not spoken the language since her mother died and it took a moment for her to switch to English. "Did Neil tell you about me?"

"Not precisely. He asked about the lineage and I guessed."

"Did you know my mother?"

"Nay, but I was a good friend to King Richard, murdered by the lad who is now the king. Richard was a good lad, I loved him very much and he loved me. The English need you, Catlin."

"How could I be of help? I know nothing of English rule and very little of the people."

"All you need to be is Charlet's daughter and I can teach you the rest. Richard tried to find your mother, but…"

"Jessup, do forgive me but I can think of nothing but freeing the Camerons. Perhaps after that is settled I will consider what to do about England."

"I understand, but please promise you will consider it. England's new king is just as evil as the men who hold the Camerons captive. Both need someone to save them and it appears God has chosen you." When Jessup's baby began to fuss, she excused herself and headed home to feed him.

*

Neil was beside himself with rage and had begun to pace from one end of the great hall to the other. His twenty most trusted men kept quiet and watched him, some sipping wine, some sitting at the table and some standing or perched on the colorful, well-stuffed pillows along the walls.

Suddenly, Neil stopped and looked at all the faces until his eyes rested on Thomas. "How many lads guard Laird Cameron?"

"Twenty-five by day and the same by night, but there are others who stand guard both within and outside the fence. The total is closer to seventy, all told. "

"If we attack, what will happen?"

"The guards will fight us. They are fond of their generous pay."

"And the lads who do not protect him? What will they do?"

"They will help us, but they have few weapons save those he sends with the hunters. Cousin, our best hope is to draw them out."

"Draw them out how?"

"That, I cannot guess. Shoes, perhaps?" He instantly realized it was not a laughing matter and regretted his remark until Neil smiled.

"It is not a bad idea. What else does the lad covet?"

"Wine, jewels, women, shoes, soft English linen, and the king of Scotland's horse." That remark brought a few chuckles from the men, but this time Neil was not impressed. "Forgive me, Cousin. What I mean is, he is as greedy as he is callous. Anything will tempt him, but he will not come out himself to get it. He will send his lads."

"I see." Neil paced back and forth a few more times before he stopped again. "I believe I have thought of something he will come out for."

*

He was taking only five men with him and just before Neil mounted his horse, he had one more stop to make. He walked up the path, knocked on the door of his oldest and dearest friends and waited for Dugan to answer. As soon as the door opened, Mayze went into his arms. He held her tight and kissed the top of her head.

"You have come for it?" Dugan asked. When Neil nodded, both Dugan and Mayze smiled. "It is ready." Dugan pointed to a flask hanging high on a peg above the door. "We feared the children would get to it."

Neil reached up, unhooked the flask and felt the fullness. "You have done very well and I am pleased."

"Will it be enough?" Mayze asked.

"It will indeed."

"We would like to go with you," said Mayze.

Neil hugged her again and then stood back. "I would like nothing better, but one war is enough. Dugan is our best hunter and I need him here to see the clan is fed." He locked forearms with Dugan and left. As soon as he returned to the courtyard, he kissed Glenna one more time and promised to be back as soon as possible. Then he mounted his horse and led the men down the valley.

Just as he expected, Catlin and Julia were near the bottom of the glen waiting with their own provisions on their horses. Catlin's hair was tied back and her determination was fierce. He stopped, looked her in the eye and finally nodded. "It will be a hard ride and we will not wait for you."

Thomas grinned. "Most likely, it is you who will have difficulty keeping up with either of them. Vengeance drove them here and it will hurry them back."

*

The ride was indeed hard. Neil took Slade, husband of Edana, with him, who had an aunt and uncle living north of the Camerons and knew the fastest way. He also took Hannish, husband of Bethia, who had slipped into the Ferguson hold undetected to do away with that man who had betrayed them. Vallam was skilled in making sounds such as a baby's cry and Luag's job was to protect Catlin. He needn't have bothered, for wherever Catlin was, Vallam was also. In only four days they were nearly there. To his surprise, the women did indeed keep up, did not complain and gained the admiration of all the men. Still, he was concerned about them and just before they were about to approach the home of Slade's aunt and uncle, Neil decided to hide them in a small clearing in the forest where they could rest. The men built a small fire and then filled a pot with water, dried meat and vegetables. Then rested while it cooked.

Neil sat down between Catlin and Thomas. "There is one thing that concerns me. Once we rid the clan of their laird and his son, who is ready to take command?"

Catlin did not have to think about that twice, "Thomas."

"Me? What did I do to make you wish such a thing on me?"

Her eyes sparkled in the firelight. "Would you like the long list or the short one?"

Thomas puffed his cheeks. "I am not a leader. Leaders know what to do and I do not."

Catlin argued, "You think too little of yourself and admit it, you were grieved to leave Dara behind. She will make you a good wife and you will take very good care of the Camerons."

"I do favor Dara and when we return home, which I remind you is with the MacGreagors, I will bring her with me."

"If she is willing," Julia reminded him.

This time he ignored his sister. "And I do not at all look kindly on the prospect of fighting the MacDonalds when they again get greedy for land? Nay, I prefer an easy life as a cobbler with the MacGreagors."

Secretly, Neil had no intention of losing the three of them and he was pleased Thomas declined. He waited too long to recover his family and hated the thought of a separation. He doubted Vallam was likely to give Catlin up anytime soon either. "Who then?"

Neither of them had an answer but for the next hour they brought up names, discussed them and decided against each. Some were too old, too young, too weak, too addle brained and all were better suited for other responsibilities.

Neil frowned. "This will not do. We cannot simply leave them with no one."

Thomas shrugged. "At least we have a few more hours to think of someone."

CHAPTER VIII

Her name was Thanna and it was to her Lammond Cameron came at night when he could not conquer any other woman. She intensely hated him and often contemplated ways to do him in, but she was not yet ready to die, as she surely would, if she killed Laird Cameron's son. At first, she felt sorry for him. He was not pleasing to look at with dark eyes, excessive eyebrows that met in the middle and a nose that resembled a hook. But her pity lasted only as long as his first unkind touch.

She sometimes submitted to other men as well in trade for food and jewels when she could get them. Someday she would escape and use the jewels to secure her sanctuary with another clan far, far away.

Thanna dreamed of it daily, so when a man she had seen only a few times before knocked on her door that evening, she let him in hoping he would offer a jewel. Even a small one would do. But this man came from the north and was not there for the usual purpose. Instead, he wanted to talk and the more he talked the more her eyes lit up. Before he left, he handed her a small bag of itching power and told her it was a gift from Laird MacGreagor.

For the first time in her life, Thanna prayed Lammond would come to her and in the darkest hour of night, her prayers were answered. She endured him and then stroked the side of his face as she always did until he fell asleep. As patiently as she could, she waited for his snoring. The louder the snore the more sound asleep he was and when she thought it was safe, she carefully got out of bed.

In the faint light of her only candle, she quietly picked his clothing up off the floor and noted exactly where his sword and dagger were so she could replace everything exactly the way it was. As she laid his clothing on the table, she glanced at him repeatedly, but he did not move. It took every ounce of her courage, but Thanna pulled the small cloth sack off the shelf, opened it and began to spread the itching power on the inside of his shirt and kilt.

*

Just after dawn and just as they hoped, Lammond and his guard raced toward the loch. Hidden in the bushes, the MacGreagors smiled at Lammond's constant scratching. It was enough to drive even the sanest man daft and each of them were determined to make his discomfort last as long as possible.

Neil waited until he was almost to the edge of the water, then he signaled and the three men were surrounded by MacGreagors wearing their old blue colors.

Lammond caught his breath and sank to his knees. "Kill them!" he ordered. But his two man guard did not move. Instead, they gawked at Neil as though he was a ghost.

"Draw your swords," Neil commanded.

The guards knew they were about to die. They watched Neil move away and two of the MacGreagors move in to face them. At least they would die honorably in a fair fight. Reluctantly, they withdrew their swords from their sheaths and soon it was over.

Lammond's breathing was heavy as he searched Neil's eyes to see what was coming next. Then he saw them. Standing behind the giants were Thomas, Julia and Catlin dressed in their Cameron colors. Catlin had a sword in her hand, walked between the men and did not stop until the tip of her sword touched Lammond's open shirt at the chest.

"I have come back to kill you, Lammond."

"No," he moaned. He scratched his groin with one hand and his back with the other, twisting to reach farther. Then a tear rolled down his cheek. "I do not want to die."

"I did not want you to touch me either." She watched more tears roll down his cheeks and soon he was sobbing and scratching all at the same time. She desperately wanted to run him through, but she could not. Instead of the fearsome hunter who kept her and all the other women on constant guard, he was now nothing more than a pathetic excuse for a man. She realized killing him would make her equally as evil, so Catlin turned, gave the sword back to Thomas and walked away.

Neil was relieved and this time, she let him take her into his arms. "Can you manage the rest of it?"

"Aye." She smiled up at him, "I am not afraid now." She quickly hugged him again and then hurried back toward the village.

Catlin was all alone and unarmed when she walked down the tree-lined road and approached the tall wooden gate with her hands clasped behind her back. Mindful of her safety, she remained just far enough away to keep the Cameron men from easily grabbing her.

The whole of the village was enclosed by a tall, wooden fence made of slats tied together with leather and reinforced with more slats held in place by wooden pegs. For a moment, she shuddered at the thought of being trapped inside again and had to remind herself Lammond was not there. She spotted one and then a second guard peeking over the top of the fence and was certain they noticed her.

Catlin heard someone shout her name.

Even so, it seemed the guards let her stand there for a long time before the gates finally began to open. When they did, there stood before her Laird Cameron himself with seven guards on either side of him. He looked a lot like his son with yellow hair, bushy eyebrows and a hooked nose.

She often counted the jewels he wore nearly everywhere a man could think to put them. He had them on his fingers, his wrists, around his neck, in his dagger, in the handle of his sword, on his belt and even sewn into the tops of his shoes. Catlin hated him for that alone. How much better he might have provided for the clan, were he willing to part with just a few of the smaller ones.

His smile was sinister and his eyes were narrowed, but she did not let him upset her. She steadied her resolve and began to shout. "I should not have run away and I offer jewels to pay my atonement."

The Cameron smirked. "I will see these jewels."

She withdrew her hands, opened the small cloth sack and pulled out the large ruby that Bethia pried out of the English necklace she had taken from her cousin some months back.

It was the largest ruby he had ever seen and Laird Cameron's eyes lit up, "Give it to me!"

"Not until I have spoken to your son for I have grieved him as well."

The Cameron glanced from side to side but his guards only

shrugged. "Find him!" Three of his men scrambled in different direction.

Catlin waited. Behind their laird, a few people dared to peek around their cottages and she could see the glee on their faces as they darted back to spread the word. If all was going according to plan, Thanna was spreading the word too and the men who were not on the side of Laird Cameron were happily preparing to carry out her instructions. All Thanna needed to say to gain their cooperation was -- "MacGreagors."

Soon his guards were back; each claiming Lammond was nowhere to be found. Laird Cameron spat on the ground, "Bloody hell, where could the laddie have got to now?" he yelled.

Catlin shouted, "Oh, then it was Lammond I saw going to the loch."

Laird Cameron nodded and six of his guards raced out the gate, turned and ran toward the loch. "And do not come back without him!"

Again they waited, Catlin standing on the outside and Laird Cameron pacing on the inside of the gate, but his guards did not come back. Laird Cameron suspected something was greatly amiss, but who would be brave enough to attack him? He stopped his pacing and turned to look into the village. Some of the people were beginning to gather, but he cared not about them. His night guards had gone home for their rest, and just in case it was a trap he needed them. "Call out the rest of my guards!" he shouted.

His shout was repeated throughout the village and his grumbling night guards staggered back out of beds, dressed and armed themselves. But when they tried, they could not open their doors. For the better part of half an hour, the clansmen had been shoving carts in front of doors and then piling belongings in them, to add the needed weight.

Laird Cameron's best men were trapped with no way out.

Mystified when his night guards did not come to help him, Laird Cameron grumbled, moaned and contemplated what to do next. He had less than ten men left to protect him. Yet he wanted the jewels and was not inclined to let unfounded fear prevent him from having them. It was, after all, just one woman. He started to charge Catlin, got almost out of the gate and stopped. Cautiously, he scanned the trees on either side of the road, peeked around one side of the fence and then the other. No one was there. Emboldened, he straightened and stepped out.

Catlin was terrified, but she held her position until he came closer and his guard was, at last, outside the gate. Then an arrow pierced Laird Cameron's heart and he fell dead at her feet. She instantly turned and ran. His guards drew their swords but when they saw the MacGreagors ride out of the trees, they panicked.

Some tried to run back inside the gate, only to find several men coming toward them with boards in their hands determined to bash their skulls in. The guards turned again and tried to escape in other directions, but they were too late. In a clash of swords, the MacGreagors soon brought them down until they lay lifeless on the ground near their laird.

There came an odd silence then and one by one, the clan's people came out of the gate to see for themselves that the evil had been cleansed from their midst. At first, they were shocked and afraid to believe their eyes. But at the sight of Julia and Catlin coming out of the trees, they began to shout for joy. Soon the grateful people were touching the MacGreagors and hugging, Julia, Catlin and Thomas.

"What about Lammond?" shouted Thanna.

Catlin hurried to her and then lovingly touched the side of her face. "You, more than any of us, have suffered his torture. We saved him for you."

CHAPTER IX

Vallam ran back, untied him, pulled Lammond out of the trees and shoved him toward the crowd. His itching increased, he walked funny holding his legs close together in an effort to scratch one with the other and even when Vallam made him stand still, he used first one foot and then another to scratch the areas where the itching powder had spread downward. He hands flew from his groin to his back, his chest to his buttocks and he was beginning to bleed from his unmerciful scratching.

Some in the crowd started to laugh, but Thanna could think of nothing but his brutality. She picked up a stone, threw it and hit him in the jaw. Then another woman picked up a stone. Her arm was stronger, her aim was better and the rock slammed into his nose causing him to stagger back and cry out in pain.

But Neil raised his hand before any more women could stone him. "It is not an easy thing for a woman to bear the guilt of having killed someone. He deserves to be executed, but the lads will see to it."

"Thank you, MacGreagor!" a man shouted. Other men joined in and soon the crowd cheered.

Again Neil raised his hand. "There is much to do. First, we must bury the dead, then you must choose a new laird and if the women are so inclined, we would appreciate a fine meal."

"It will be a feast!" Catlin shouted. She gathered her skirts and hurried inside the gate followed by all but one of the women. Thanna grabbed one more rock, hurled it at Lammond and then darted away.

"We want you to be our Laird, MacGreagor. You could come home and we could combine our two clans." The lad's request was met with emphatic nods from the other Cameron men and slaps on the back.

Neil smiled. "We have a new home now and it is very pleasing. However, I might suggest someone to lead you. He is a strong lad who is fair minded, trained in the ways of the MacGreagors and just as capable of leading you as I am."

"Who?"

"His name is Luag MacGreagor." Neil quickly turned to see the look of total surprise on Luag's face. "You have been my away second for many months and you are an honorable lad. Stay with them at least until they find another. Who knows, perhaps you might prefer them and they might decide to keep you. If not, you always have a home with us."

Luag scratched the side of his beard that was just beginning to grow long enough and then looked at the faces of the eager Camerons. "Do all of you agree?" He was surprised when they nodded and somewhere inside he found the opportunity exciting. "Then I will stay for now."

"What is your first command?" asked Neil.

Luag did not hesitate. "Gather your weapons and bring the guards out. None who have sided with Laird Cameron will be allowed to live."

In a rush, the men obeyed, first running inside the Keep to get their swords and then to the cottages where their captives waited. Some of the captives, they noticed, managed to escape and run away. But in the end, they marched seventeen unarmed men, with their hands tied behind their backs, out through the gates. Two men picked up the weeping Lammond and dragged him off with the others to be executed near the Cameron cemetery.

Finally, it was finished.

*

The evening meal was indeed a feast, the people drank and danced to the music of a flute, the children played and every face had a smile on it.

"It is fresh air like no other," Catlin said.

Vallam did not realize she was standing next to him and he turned to smile at her. "I can only imagine what it was like before." He watched the dancing, and then two boys chasing each other caught his attention. "Catlin, will you walk with me?"

"Aye." By his side, she walked through the open gate and started down the road.

He wanted to take her hand, but he had not touched her since the day she ran into his arms and he was unsure she would welcome it. Instead, he clasped his hands behind his back. Often in their travels, she looked at him, but that was all and he had no way of knowing if she felt anything for him other than gratitude. Still, he had to know before it drove him daft. "What will you do now?"

She did not quickly answer. "I am torn. These are my people and I love them, yet…"

"Go on."

"The MacGreagors have fine new land with less possibility of war, or so it seems. I detest war almost as much as I detest lads who cry."

He nodded. "I confess I am not fond of lads who cry either and the MacGreagors would cast out any lad who does. We cannot afford weakness."

"That is what I mean. It is far more pleasing for a lass to be surrounded by strong lads on good land, who will see they have strong and healthy children. Even the hunting is better there."

"You could always come back to visit the Camerons from time to time."

"True, there is that."

"Then you will go back with us?"

She had a twinkle in her eye when she answered. "Aye." Then she remembered there was still the unresolved question and her smile faded. Did she want to be the Queen of England? Did she have a choice in the matter, after all, if that situation was not resolved, the king would continue to look for her. If only she had someone to talk to, someone she could trust who would help her think it through.

She promised Neil she would not tell anyone, but that was only to protect her and she was sure Vallam would do nothing to bring her harm. Besides, how long could it be before her secret was known? Already there were four MacGreagors who knew and if Neil remembered who her mother really was, then others must as well.

Suddenly, she grabbed Vallam's hand. "Come with me."

He was thrilled she wanted to touch him. But then she took him to the cemetery, which was not his idea of a good place to spend a fine

Scottish evening. At least she passed the new graves and headed down the hill toward the older ones. She let go of his hand, plucked two wild flowers out of the ground and laid one on a grave. "This is where my father rests." She moved to the next grave and laid the other flower down. "And this is my mother." She turned to closely watch his face. "My mother's name was Bridget Cameron."

Catlin saw no flicker of recognition in his eyes. "Her name was also, "Charlet.""

Vallam's mouth dropped open. "The lass who turned down the throne of England?"

"Aye." She paused to let him get used to the idea. "They tell me she turned it down to marry my father."

"They must have loved each other a great deal."

"That is what they tell me. I have yet to know that kind of love, but I hope someday to find it."

"So do I." This time he looked deep into her eyes hoping to see some reaction, but there was none so he looked away. Perhaps she did have a heart of stone as Thomas said.

"Have you heard the king of England is looking for Charlet?"

"Aye."

"He means to kill her. But once more my mother robs them of their English desires." Catlin found a log and sat down. "However…"

"Catlin, are you saying the English will search for you?"

"I am the only remaining child. The smaller graves are those of my brothers and sisters, all lost in the plague."

He was stunned and hardly knew what to say. "What do you intend to do?"

"Therein lies the problem. I do not know. Have you a suggestion?"

He managed to seat himself next to her, stretch out his legs and fold his arms before he answered. "Your mother hid successfully, perhaps you can also."

"Aye but what kind of life can it be? Always I would wonder if the English were coming." Catlin unexpectedly giggled, "Mother was so protective of us I thought she was half out of her mind. Now, of course, I understand why and I do not want to do that to my children? I can think of no other answer than to face the English and resolve this issue once and for all."

He did not know what to say and for a time they sat together on the log, each lost in thought until the sun began to set and Catlin stood up. "So you see, it would not be wise for a Highlander to fall in love with me."

He stood up also and bowed his head. "But for this Highlander, it is too late."

She was not surprised. Anyone could see how he felt about her. "Please, do not make this more difficult than it already is." Catlin turned and walked away.

CHAPTER X

Anxious to get home, the MacGreagors stayed only two more days to make sure all was set for Luag to take over. Early on the morning of the third day, Neil visited the place where his Aunt Rachel and Uncle Connor were buried. Then they all went to see what happened to the old MacGreagor home.

Just as Thomas said, it was haunted. As soon as they rode to the top of the hill where they could look down into the small valley they stopped. It was so quiet, it truly did unnerve Neil. Even the birds seemed to have lost their song. Everything inside the wall still looked burned except for a few plants that managed to break through the rubble to begin new life. What was left of the Keep and the wall appeared to be slowly crumbling. The cottages in the distance were deserted and there was not a man, woman, child or animal in sight.

However, there was one very apparent change. It appeared the MacDonalds finally managed to divert the water, causing the moat to completely dry up and the loch in the distance to become little more than a creek. Neil smiled and wondered just how long the English would hold their ire over the lack of water flowing to them.

At length, he led the others down the hill and once he found the path, he turned toward the graveyard. It might have been a far more somber occasion had Julia and Thomas not been arguing.

"Aye, but where is Dara?" Julia taunted. "You said you would make her your wife and bring her with us."

Thomas puffed his cheeks. "She is otherwise detained."

"Detained how?"

"I do not care to say."

Neil dismounted and was relieved to find the graves of his beloved family had not been disturbed. For just a moment, he stood in front of Anna's place of rest, bowed his head and said a prayer, during which everyone was quiet. However, the second he finished crossing himself and lifted his head, the argument continued.

Thomas glared at his sister, "If you must know, I did not marry Dara because her husband would not let me."

Neil laughed and got back on his horse. "I see no reason to linger here, we…"

"I do," Thomas countered.

"What?"

"I found the most wonderful apple tree when…"

"I forgot about the apple tree." It took only a few moments to ride across the meadow and the road, and then turn up the path to the loch. Still seated on their horses and thrilled with the find, all the MacGreagors began to fill their sacks with ripe, red apples.

"I just thought of something," Thomas said once they left the old land of the MacGreagors and headed home. "Do you suppose by now rumor has reached Laird MacDonald and he is cowering under his bed convinced the MacGreagor ghost will come for him next?"

*

For Vallam, there was no greater torture than being near Catlin and not being able to touch her. At night as they made their way home he often laid on his side facing her just in case she reached out. But she did not. Occasionally, she glanced at him but just as quickly looked away. It was obvious she meant what she said and his heart was breaking.

*

He thought it would be better once they were home, but it was not. Catlin was so close yet so far from him and at times, he thought he would lose his mind. There was nothing to do but keep busy, so he trained with Walrick, helped build the cottages and then collapsed into bed hoping to sleep. But even sleep eluded him and every night he turned on his side to face the direction he knew her to be.

Catlin avoided Vallam and with Luag gone, she rarely went for a walk. But there were still occasions when they met on a path and she could not help but look into his eyes. She saw just a glint of sadness and it hurt her to know she could not ease his pain.

Still, her decision was not yet made. Daily, it seemed there was word of some new atrocity the English king brought down on his own people and Jessup was anxious for her to reveal herself to the world. But the question of how precisely to do that without endangering all of Scotland had no answer. The weight of two nations rested squarely on her shoulders and she hated every bit of it. Even Neil could not guess what to do.

Slipping into England was not the problem, protection once she got there was. She would need an army capable of overthrowing the king's men and although possible, it would take considerable time to gather one. To build an army, she would need to reveal who she was and that would only encourage the English king to seek her out and try to kill her.

The real question was, as Jessup pointed out, -- being half-English, did Catlin care enough about the English children to risk her life? It would have been a far easier decision had Jessup not mentioned children and Catlin's heart was truly divided.

Perhaps the answer might have come more easily if Catlin could concentrate, but she thought only of Vallam -- his touch, his voice, his arms around her and the look she saw in his eyes. His eyes haunted her until she thought she would lose her mind. Only at night when she could turn on her side and face the direction she knew him to be, could she find any comfort at all.

Every waking moment she charged herself to make up her mind, but she could not. One thing she knew for sure, she would never pass this curse down to her children. Going to England was the only way to be done with it, even if it cost Catlin her life. Her mind knew it to be true, but her heart simply would not allow her to leave.

Then a messenger came from the land of the MacPhearson with the news. It was confirmed, the new king of England was dead, murdered in his bed by a woman. As soon as she heard, Catlin turned on her heels and started to run. She went first to Vallam's cottage, but he was not there. She raced down the path to the end of the cottages, shielded her eyes from the bright sunlight and then scanned the men in training with Walrick. Again, he was not there. She could not think what to do next and was about to head off in another direction when she heard his voice behind her.

"Please say you are looking for me."

Catlin turned and threw herself into his strong arms. "Have you heard? England has a new king and Jessup says he is a good lad. I am free finally and I do love you. I love you very much." She felt his arms tighten around her and then he begin to swing her around. Soon she was laughing and crying at the same time. So great was her joy, she kissed his neck repeatedly.

Then he stopped and looked down into the glorious green eyes that were finally his.

Slowly he lowered his lips to hers.

-end-

LASHA

CHAPTER I

Cowan heard the faint cry of what he thought might be a child. The sun was high in the sky, a welcome sight after two days of rain, and for the last hour, he had been following the muddy tracks of several deer. At first when he heard the cry he thought it was a cat for they often made that sort of sound, but as he grew closer he feared otherwise. He had gone farther south than he normally did on the hunt, had not seen anyone else since early morning and if it was a child it was certainly a long way from home.

Finally close enough, Cowan MacGreagor cautiously slid down off his horse and tied his stallion to the branch of a tree. He was well aware he could be walking into a trap and pulled his dagger just in case. It would not be the first time the imitation of a child's cry drew a man to his death. Slowly and quietly he eased through the thick forest foliage and crept closer to the sound.

Abruptly the crying stopped.

Cowan quickly crouched behind a bush and waited. Then the crying began again and this time the child cried out for its mother. At least now, he knew for certain it was a child. Determined, he glanced around to make sure he was not about to be attacked and then started forward again until he could see the top of the child's head.

Once more, he crouched down behind a bush and then he slowly parted it to get a better look. It was a boy of not more than two or three with tears streaking down his dirty face -- and he was hopelessly stuck. The loose threads of his kilt were tangled in a bush and it appeared the more the boy struggled, the more his kilt came unraveled and wound around the bush.

Still concerned it was a trap, Cowan glanced around once more, stood up, hurried to the child and quickly cut him free. Then he scooped the boy into his arms and swiftly carried him back to his horse. He wanted to set the boy down to check for injuries, but the boy had his little arms around Cowan's neck and was desperately clinging to him.

"There now laddie, you are safe." Cowan tried to set him down again, but still the little boy would not let go and for a man who loved children and wanted many of his own, it was the greatest feeling in the world.

Cowan was a man of large stature with wavy, shoulder length blond hair which he normally wore tied back. His eyes were blue, his face was oval-shaped and he prided himself on keeping his beard and mustache neatly trimmed. He was a MacGreagor and he wore the predominately green kilt of his clan, but the little boy did not. Instead, he wore the red kilt of a Haldane.

Most MacGreagors believed there was something amiss with the Haldanes for in all the months since they came to live in the valley, the Haldanes had not spoken a word to any of them. Haldane warriors were often seen in the forest watching the MacGreagors, particularly when they practiced their warrior skills, but never had they come close enough to speak. They did not appear to be hostile either so the MacGreagors just let them watch.

Just the same, such quiet neighbors were unsettling and Neil often sent men to watch them too. That was before they discovered how small in numbers the Haldane were. Some guessed as few as forty not counting the children, yet they were a lively bunch and always the scouts came back with entertaining stories of what they had seen.

Not all the MacGreagors believed the wild stories and Cowan was one of them. His first thought was to take the boy to Laird MacGreagor, but the Haldane might think he kidnapped him, so the only answer was to take him home.

Cowan continued to rub the little boy's back to calm him down, "Are you thirsty?" He felt the nod and this time when he tried to set him down the boy let go. He untied his water flask and by the way the boy greedily drank and the way he smelled, it was clear he had been lost for quite a while. It was also clear the child was about to go to sleep so Cowan put away the flask. He pulled an extra plaid out of his sack, wrapped the child up, set him on the horse and then swung up behind him. A full hour later, he urged his horse up to the crest of a hill, stopped and got his first look at the Haldane village.

The Haldane lived in a valley too, although it was much smaller as was their village. The one-story keep was in the center of less than thirty cottages. By the different colors of stone and mortar, it was obvious rooms had been added to the Keep at various times over the years.

Not far from the laird's home stood a stable, several store houses and an odd structure Cowan heard about but did not truly believe existed. The structure was little more than a wooden frame but in the center hung a large, rusted, square plate of iron. Next to it, hung a piece of wood shaped somewhat like Cowan's forearm with a wad of cloth tied around the thickest end.

A flock of sheep and several cattle dotted the bottom half of the valley and the people were going about their business as usual except for one thing -- there seemed to be few men to guard them. Cowan found some comfort in that. If they believed he was hostile, he would have fewer Haldane to fight.

But just as he started to urge his horse down the hill a woman screamed. It alarmed Cowan. He quickly halted and tried to see if he could tell where the scream came from. A second later, a man backed out of the Keep and ducked just in time to avoid a wooden bowl someone inside hurled at him. This time the woman's scream sounded more like a command and Cowan was surprised. Perhaps the rumors of the Haldane's ill-mannered wife were true after all.

Cowan checked the bundle in his lap, saw that the boy was still sound asleep and put the cloth back over the child's head. He waited a few moments until he believed the woman had calmed and then continued on down the hillside. As soon as he broke through the trees, someone shouted and three men, including the one who backed out of the Keep, drew their swords. Their glares were fierce and they looked prepared for battle, but Cowan did not pause. Instead, he walked his horse into the valley and headed straight for the men.

The shout of his approach roused the clan and soon two more men and several women gathered in the courtyard. But Cowan kept his eyes on the man in the middle whom he guessed was Laird Haldane and when he was near enough, he halted, turned his horse to the side and lifted the cloth off the boy's head.

The small crowd erupted into shouts of joy.

"You have found him!" A woman with tears welling up in her eyes ran to Cowan. But just a couple of feet away she slipped in the mud and fell on her backside. Suddenly her tears turned to shrieks of laughter, which made everyone else laugh. He could not help but like this woman and he did think the sight funny, but he kept his face emotionless. It was one thing for her clan to laugh at her, but quite another for a stranger to do so.

Nevertheless, he quickly dismounted and with the boy in one arm, he reached out his hand to her. "Are you hurt?"

"Nay." She held his hand with both of hers, let him pull her up and then took the boy out of his arms. "Thank you." She smiled, waited just a moment for his nod and then dashed back to the three men. Each quickly put his sword away and lovingly touched the child before she took him inside the Keep.

Had she not been the mother and no doubt a wife, Cowan might have been even more taken with the woman. She had long, dark eyelashes that matched the color of her hair, which she let freely hang down her back to her waist. Her voice was like music when she laughed and she had dimples, one in each cheek when she smiled. He watched her disappear inside and was ready to get back on his horse when the three men boldly came closer.

CHAPTER II

"I am Laird Haldane," said the older man in the middle. His hair and clothing were disheveled, he looked tired and he was about to say something more when a woman inside the Keep started yelling.

"You miserable excuse for a husband, I told you to keep watch over the laddie. Look at him, he is filthy and he smells. I blame you, husband, for …"

Completely humiliated, Laird Haldane did not say a word. He only frowned, blinked repeatedly and then held his eyes to the top of his head waiting for her to stop.

"You are the devil's own son, you are," the woman continued. "Little more than a scunner, to my way of thinking."

Laird Haldane winced when she called him a scunner. Finally, it was quiet for a moment. He again opened his mouth to speak and got but three words out before she began again. This time Laird Haldane simply sighed and tried to talk over her yelling. "Are you married?"

"Nay," Cowan admitted.

"I do not recommend it. She will run down in a while and then she will bathe her sore throat in wine and become far more friendly. I was deceived when I married, you see. I loved her and love can be very deceiving. At the time, she was quiet without many words. She has changed."

"Why do you allow it?"

"Unfortunately, I love that lass still. Love can be persuasive even after the wedding night."

Cowan was confused. The woman who came to get the boy cried, then laughed and was now yelling? She was clearly daft and he felt sorry for the Haldanes. He did not know what to say, so he simply nodded.

"I thank you for bringing my son home. He is my only child whom I love very much." Laird Haldane rolled his eyes and paused to listen once more to the incessant yelling of his wife. Her name calling included scallywag, beast and demon, but the worst of them was scunner and once more Laird Haldane winced.

Cowan glanced at the other men and each looked just as perturbed as their laird. Then the yelling stopped. To his surprise, the woman who came to get the boy appeared in the doorway of the Keep and was smiling. How was it possible for a woman to change her disposition so quickly? He could not believe his eyes. "Is she daft?"

Laird Haldane quickly looked to see who the MacGreagor warrior was talking about and when he turned back, he too was smiling. "That is not my wife. She is, Lasha, my sister and I would that all women had her temperament. It is my wife, Ena, who yells. She can be very entertaining and good company when she has a mind to … when she is not yelling … which I admit is rare these days."

The women in the courtyard seemed fascinated by Cowan's size, but his gaze kept drifting back to Lasha. He had to think of something to say to take his mind and his eyes off her. "Why have you not come to see Laird MacGreagor? He is a good lad and he will welcome you."

Laird Haldane moved a little closer and leaned toward Cowan. "It is my wife, you see. I cannot leave her and I cannot take her with me.

Does Laird MacGreagor truly have a golden sword?"

Cowan was caught completely off guard by the question and at a loss for words. He detested lying but in this case, he had no choice. "I have never seen one." It was true; he had not yet come to the glen when the sword was last seen and now no one knew where it was, save Neil.

"I am grieved indeed. I had my heart set on seeing one. Oh, I nearly forgot." He nodded to one of his men who quickly ran to the odd structure with the iron plate. The man untied the large wooden baton, grabbed hold of the smaller end with both hands, backed up and struck the plate as hard as he could. The sound spooked his horse and Cowan had to hold the stallion's halter down to keep him for bolting.

"Forgive me, I should have warned you. It calls our searchers back, you see. I hear tell you use whistles. We use the Bonnie there to alert our clan. Perhaps someday you will tell us about the different whistles."

Cowan had heard that sound before, but never knew what it was. For weeks, he suspected it was some fearsome animal they had not yet encountered, and was glad to learn it was not. "I fear my laird would not approve my giving away all our secrets."

Laird Haldane stroked his straggly beard thoughtfully. "I suppose he would not, at that."

The yelling started again and Cowan studied the pained look on Laird Haldane's face for a moment. "My father's third wife carried on like that, but he tamed her."

Haldane's eyes lit up as did those of the other men. "How?"

"He put her out and would not let her back in until she stopped yelling. It might take a time or two, but once you put a lass out in the rain, she begins to see reason."

"What did he do about the name calling?"

"I believe he kept half a goblet of water handy and threw it in her face when her words disturbed him. I caution you, she will soon learn to duck. Before father got her tamed, the water hit me more often than it did her."

Haldane chuckled. "I will keep that in mind. Are you quite certain there is no golden sword?"

Cowan was about to answer when Lasha boldly walked up to him.

"I thank you for bringing my nephew home." She put her arms around his neck, gently pulled his head down and lightly kissed his lips. Then she let go and stood back.

Cowan quickly looked to see if he was about to die, but Laird Haldane was still smiling. He got back on his horse, looked once more at Lasha and then rode back the way he came.

When he reached the crest of the hill, he stopped, turned his horse and looked back. All of the Haldanes were still watching him, but his eyes went to Lasha.

*

Lasha hurried across the great hall to her small bedchamber in the back of the Keep and closed the door so she could change out of her muddy clothing. Unlike the larger bedchamber her parents afforded her as a child, this one was hardly big enough for a bed. She might have been in the larger one still, but when the boy finished nursing,

Ena demanded that room for her son. Therefore, Haldane had another room added on to the back for her. Lasha did not mind. This room was small but it was far enough away to keep her from hearing Ena's voice, unless it was excessively loud…and that was a very good thing.

Lasha could not seem to stop thinking about the MacGreagor. It was not as though she had never seen a MacGreagor before. Sometimes when she rode north to watch the swans on the loch, she went further still, hid in the forest and watched them from afar. But she had never seen that particular MacGreagor or she would have remembered.

She meant it only as a gesture of gratitude, but when she touched him and felt the softness of his lips, she found her attraction to him perplexing. All her life she assumed she would marry within her own clan. In fact, her brother sometimes mentioned his desire for her to do just that and for a very good reason -- the Haldane clan was small and in order for it to grow, the women needed to stay.

Lasha wondered if it meant her brother felt the Haldane men incapable of finding wives outside the clan. Perhaps they were not the most handsome men in all the world, but neither were they *that* ill-favored. But her brother was also her laird and she did not often question his reasoning except on one subject -- Ena. Why her brother loved that woman was a secret known only to God.

Living with her sister-in-law was sometimes misery and were it not for her brother's love, her delight in her nephew and her ability to block out the sound of Ena's voice most of the time, Lasha might have seriously considered marriage sooner. She had already turned down two proposals and that left only three unmarried men in the clan, none of which were older than she. One was even two years younger and at fourteen, he was not even fully-grown.

Of the three, there was one man she found attractive enough. Sionn was pleasant, easy to look at and considerate of the woman. He was also very strong -- or at least she thought so until the MacGreagor so easily pulled her to her feet after she fell in the mud -- and with only one hand. Lasha smiled at the memory.

She quickly removed her soiled plaid, pleated her clean, dry one and rushed back to the great hall. Now that the boy was clean, she gathered up his soiled kilt and the MacGreagor plaid the stranger had him wrapped in. What better excuse to see the MacGreagor again than to return his plaid? She smiled, went out the door and walked down the path to the creek. Usually, one of the other women did the wash for the laird's family, but today she wanted make sure it was spotlessly clean.

She dipped the wool kilt in the water, began to rub soap on it and then abruptly stopped. The creek was not wide and when the shadow of a man blocked out the light on the cloth, it quickly got her attention. She glanced up, saw that it was Sionn and motioned for him to move aside. When he didn't, she stood up. "Is something amiss?"

"Lasha, I have come to ask you to marry me." He spread his legs apart, folded his arms and waited.

"Oh. I confess I have been expecting it."

"There are but four women for me to choose from and you are the eldest. I choose you."

"I am flattered."

She did not continue and he looked unsettled. "What is your

answer?"

Yesterday...this morning even, she would have said yes but now there was suddenly another possibility. In fact, just north of their hold were as many as twenty other possibilities. For the first time, Lasha took a long hard look at Sionn Haldane. He was average, she supposed -- neither pleasant nor unpleasant with average brown hair and blue eyes. He was neither too short nor too tall, too thin nor too... "I will give you my answer later."

It was not what he expected and Sionn wrinkled his brow. For most of his life he assumed he would marry within his clan and fortunate indeed would be the man who married Laird Haldane's sister. "When might I expect your answer?"

Lasha lightly bit her lower lip, "Will you wait a fortnight?" She could tell he was not pleased, neither did he seem all that disappointed, and at length he nodded and walked away.

CHAPTER III

Lasha did not mean to, but all afternoon she kept comparing Sionn to the MacGreagor. She did not even know the MacGreagor's name but she knew his lips and could not get the thought of them out of her mind. Sionn had not spoken of love nor had she expected him to. In fact, he rarely spoke to her at all over the years. He was a Haldane hunter and a good man from what she could tell. But he was not mystifying or exciting -- not at all like the short encounter with the MacGreagor. On the other hand, how would she know? Even as Sionn proposed to her, he stood on the other side of the creek and did not touch her. Perhaps she would find his touch mystifying as well…if he ever touched her.

It took a while, but Lasha worked at her washing until the garments were as clean as she knew how to make them. She wrung each out and hung it on a tree branch to dry. Hopefully, a fairly strong breeze would present itself and do most of the drying so she would not be forced to hang them near the hearth at night. Ena would surely have something unkind to say about having a MacGreagor plaid inside the Keep and Lasha was not in the mood to hear it.

*

As most clans preferred, the Haldane's great hall was big enough to hold several people at once. It had a long, narrow table in the center, chairs against the walls and a stone hearth at one end. Animal skins adorned one wall, weapons hung on another and a small, colorful, aging and fraying tapestry hung on the third. Three doors along the back wall led to adjoining bedchambers, a fourth door went to the outside and a fifth led to a kitchen.

It was an ordinary evening in the Haldane keep. Lasha's brother was happy and her sister-in-law was not. Ena was not an unpleasant woman to look at. In fact, when she smiled she might even be thought of as beautiful. The problem was, she rarely smiled. Her hair was a soft yellow which she wore in two braids in summer and loose in winter for the warmth of it. Her eyes were brown; her complexion extraordinarily soft for an older woman and her stature was graceful. If she did not have such a vile temper, Lasha might even like her.

Lasha sat across the table from her brother and Ena, ate her evening meal in silence and waited. She waited through the yelling…waited through the insults…and still she waited. Yet, when Ena called the MacGreagor a scunner, that was the end of it. Lasha abruptly stood up, shoved her chair back, put both hands on her hips and glared at her brother. "You heard the lad, put Ena out!"

The Haldane's mouth dropped. "Lasha, you have never spoken to me thusly."

"We had no answer before. I tell you now, brother, handle your wife or I will seek sanctuary with the MacGreagors." With that, she walked out the door, marched across the courtyard to her favorite tree stump in front of the elder's cottage, sat down in a huff and tightly folded her arms.

Laird Haldane could not believe his ears and quickly followed her out. "You cannot mean it. Would you truly leave us?"

"I can take no more of her bad mood. She should be grateful to have the boy back, not furious he was lost to begin with. Put her out before we all go daft." He studied the determination in her eyes, thought about it for a moment and then headed back inside the Keep.

For once his wife was speechless and her eyes nervously shifted when she saw him come through the door. In just a few short steps, he crossed the room, bent down, grabbed her behind the knees and laid her over his shoulder. "Ena, we will have no more of your yelling." He heard her draw in a sharp breath and fully expected her to hit him with her fists, but she was far too stunned. He turned, hauled her out the door and carried her to the same puddle of mud Lasha fell in earlier. Careful not to hurt her, he plopped her down and backed away.

Ena could feel the cold wetness seeping through the back of her wool plaid and her ire began to steadily rise. She pulled one hand out of the mud, then the other and flung the wet dirt at her husband. Then the full force of her rage began to show in her face. "How dare you! You will pay for this!"

The Haldane turned, motioned for Lasha to come inside and then closed the door behind him. He expected a whole string of vile words but it was quiet outside and that made him extremely nervous. He began to pace from one end of the room to the other and made three complete turns when suddenly the sound of the baton hitting the iron plate broke the silence. Again it sounded and again and again.

Haldane put both hands over his ears to block out the sound and turned to Lasha, "Now what do I do?"

"Water! The MacGreagor said…"

He rushed to the water bucket, happily found it full and as soon as Lasha opened it, he headed out the door. Outside Ena's back was to him, the sound of the ringing iron prevented her from hearing his approach and he managed to dump the full bucket of water on her head before she had the slightest inkling.

Slowly, she dropped the baton, shoved her soggy hair out of her face and turned to face him. Completely stupefied she could not find the right words to say, "How...? I mean...I am the mother of your..."

"Aye and my son will sleep much better when you have stopped that constant bellowing."

"I do not bellow. Besides it is your fault I am unhappy."

"I give you all that I have, Ena."

She bit her lip and looked as though she were about to cry, "You do not love me, you never did." As hard as she tried, she could not make the tears come. Ena decided to let her rage show instead and her voice steadily began to rise to match her irritation. "I should not have married you, you are a..."

One of the men handed Laird Haldane a new bucket of water and when he looked, the searchers were back and the whole clan was watching him. He drew in a deep breath and steadied his resolve. "Ena, there will be no more of your yelling and no more unkind language!"

She narrowed her eyes and began to clench her fists. "You would not dare..." Before she could finish her sentence, he dumped the second bucket of water on her head.

Even slower this time, she shoved the wet hair away from her face with both hands. She thought to wipe her face with the hem of her plaid, but when she looked down, it was just as wet as her face. Only then did she think of something else to say but it was too late;

her husband had already gone back inside and slammed the door.

It was then she noticed the looks on the faces of the rest of the clan. They were not laughing, but most were smiling as if to say she finally got what she deserved. She glared at one or two and soon the courtyard was empty, which left her all alone and dripping wet.

*

At sunset and after two of the most peaceful hours the clan had enjoyed in months, Laird Haldane went back outside to find his wife. He found her sitting on a log at the edge of the forest just beyond the village, and he could tell she had been genuinely crying. As soon as he helped her stand up, he pulled her into his arms. "For the life of me, I cannot understand why I love you so, but I do." He kissed her tears away and then kissed her passionately. "Are you truly that unhappy?"

"Sometimes, but I do not always know why."

"Ena, the laddie needs a happy home. Shall we not give it to him?"

She nodded and then went back into his arms.

*

Cowan MacGreagor had not gone directly home. Instead, he stayed in the forest near the Haldane village and watched. Something told him it would be long into the night before he stopped thinking about Lasha's dimples, her kiss and the way her hair smelled of wild roses.

He was pleased when she came back outside and began to wash his plaid. He had forgotten the cloth and now he had a good excuse to come back. Cowan was not very far away when the Haldane approached Lasha at the creek, yet he was too far to hear what they talked about and in the end, it did not appear to be anything serious.

The MacGreagor was also in the forest not very far away when Haldane's wife received her two buckets of water. Later, Lasha came back outside to see if the wash was dry which afforded him one last look at her. By then it was getting late and he needed to get back before Neil sent men to look for him.

He rode hard and just before the darkness fell, he dismounted in the MacGreagor courtyard and went to tell Neil about his encounter with the Haldane. The MacGreagor great hall was filled with the usual people for the evening meal. It included Neil and Glenna, the children, and Thomas and Julia. When Glenna insisted Cowan join them, he quickly consented. The bowls of mutton stew looked very enticing and smelled wonderful to a man who had forgotten to eat a noon meal.

The more Cowan talked, the more both Glenna and Neil noticed his mention of someone named Lasha. Once was normal. However, the mention of a woman's name repeatedly was a clear indication that the man was smitten. Neil exchanged knowing glances with his wife and waited until Cowan finished describing Ena's two buckets of water. He laughed and was about to speak when Thomas spoke instead.

"Is Lasha married?" Thomas looked from the shocked expression on Cowan's face to an identical one on Neil's. "Have I misspoken? You said she has dimples and I find I fancy dimples on a lass."

Any other time Cowan might have enjoyed discussing the attributes of a woman with dimples but since it involved Lasha, he somehow found the question annoying. "I…"

Julia rolled her eyes, "Do not be put out, Cowan, my brother prefers women with dimples, women without, women with any color of hair or eyes, and women of any size and shape."

Thomas looked as though he was giving the matter deep and serious thought. "It is not true; I have yet to prefer a lass with gray hair."

Finally, Cowan realized it was a joke, and the next move was his. He glanced at Neil and then stared at Thomas. "At least that is taken care of."

"What is taken care of?" asked Neil.

"I hoped you might hold a feast and invite the Haldane, but I could not think whom you might choose to act the village idiot."

Glenna and Julia erupted in laughter, Thomas frowned, Neil grinned and slowly Cowan's lips curved into a smile.

CHAPTER IV

After the evening meal and after Thomas, Julia and Cowan went to their respective beds, Neil and Glenna were about to retire to their third-story bedchamber when Ben burst through the door. With beads of sweat on his brow, Ben paused for just a second to catch his breath. "Alison is in labor!"

Any other time it would have been happy news, but of the last five women to give birth, three died taking two of the unborn babies with them and Alison, the middle child of the nine sisters, was terrified she would be the fourth.

Glenna tried to comfort him. "Do calm yourself, Ben, she will be fine."

Ben did not look convinced. "She sent me to find the priest."

Neil put a hand on Ben's shoulder. "I will find the priest; you belong with your wife."

Ben did not have to think about that for long. In a blink, he was back out the door. Neil took Glenna in his arms and kissed her forehead. "I am grateful you are not with child just now. The women are terrified and the lads are unreasonable."

"Will the lads come to place their wagers?"

"I do not expect them to…not this time, not after two women and two babes in a row died. They fear God has not looked kindly on their wagers."

"But they must come. They must celebrate loudly and convince

Alison all is as it should be."

He saw the value in her reasoning, nodded and released her. "I will gather the lads."

Just as he reached the door, Glenna made one more suggestion. "And find the priest but tell him not to come unless you send for him a second time. Let Alison fight to live long enough to receive the last rites."

She watched her husband go and went up the stairs to check on the children. Assured they were fine, she knelt by her bed to say a prayer for Alison and her baby.

Each time a woman died, Glenna and the two midwives discussed what might be going wrong, but the circumstances were so different they could detect no clear pattern in what they ate or what they did. Some women lived and some died…it was just the way of the world. Lately however, too many of the women were dying.

Even with the influx of English brides, the clan was not growing as quickly as Neil hoped. All the clans suffered diseases, injuries and plagues that could wipe out half and make them vulnerable to attack. Less than a week before, they got word of a terrible plague in France that was causing the people to go mad. Everyone prayed that plague would quietly pass them by.

Then there was the problem with the brides. Several who did not quickly fall in love chose to go back to England. Seventeen others were still unmarried. They stayed but the men seemed in less of a hurry to court them than the women were to take husbands. It was very perplexing. At times, the lack of courting irritated both Neil and Glenna, but love could not be rushed…or at least that is what they told each other.

Deep in prayer on her knees next to her bed, Glenna's eyes shot wide open. "A feast? Of course!"

*

It wasn't long until there was a burst of activity in the great hall. Neil tried to convince the men that the more normal they acted, the less the women would be afraid. It sounded reasonable, especially to the men whose wives were also in line to give birth. Neil broke out the boards so the men could place their wagers on the sex of the child while Walrick and Gelson brought their wives and then went to fetch more wine.

Knowing full well no one was going to get any sleep until Alison gave birth, the wives hurried up the stairs to be with Glenna. It was the perfect opportunity to gossip about the clan's three most important men without fear of being overheard.

*

Outside his cottage, Ben paused in his pacing to listen to the celebration noises coming from the Keep. This was his first child and he was filled with a jumble of love for Alison, pride, prayer and extreme terror. But if the other men thought everything was normal, perhaps Ben could breathe just a little easier. It helped. But then from inside the cottage Alison's moan seemed louder and longer than the one before. Ben might have gone in to check on her, but all eight of the sisters and two midwives were already in there.

There was nothing he could do but wait and he should be accustomed to it after waiting every spring for all the new animals to be born. But this was different. He could not help remembering how frightened Alison was, fearing she would die in childbirth like her mother. At the time he talked her into becoming his wife, he saw no reason to think she would take after her mother in that regard. But now…now that she was so near her time, he realized if she did die he would be to blame.

*

In the great hall, the men were only pretending to be happy. There was not a married man among them who did not know exactly how Ben was feeling and few were convinced Alison would live. Something was going dreadfully wrong with the women and the men could not think what to do about it. So on this night they sat on pillows, at the table or leaned against the wall and drank their wine. Every once in a while, Neil raised his hand; the men roared with laughter or shouted something and then quieted again.

*

The three women upstairs had become fast friends over the months and it wasn't the first time they spent an entire evening together. On some nights, they preferred it that way. Glenna poured each a portion of wine and then sat down with them at the small table in the bedchamber she shared with Neil. The women were as different as night and day. Glenna had brown hair that curled around the sides of her face, was tall and had soft blue eyes. Steppen's face was square like her brother's, her hair was golden and her eyes were dark while Jonrose also had blond hair, but her eyes were a softer brown and her smile could positively light up a room. Both Steppen and Jonrose were shorter than Glenna.

Glenna frowned, "Lorna?"

"Aye." Jonrose was the mother of four with a fifth on the way and often surprised Steppen and Glenna with her keen observations. "Lorna watches the lads but when one approaches, she walks away."

"And you believe she is so afraid of giving birth she deprives herself of love?"

"I can think of no other reason for it."

Steppen set her goblet down and let Glenna refill it. "Perhaps the right lad had not yet approached her."

"Perhaps. There is one lad she tends to notice more than the others."

Both Steppen and Glenna leaned closer. "Who?"

"Cowan."

Steppen smiled, Glenna did not. "Lorna waited too long. Cowan has his mind set on Lasha Haldane." It was the first Jonrose or Steppen heard about the latest Haldane encounter and both demanded Glenna tell them every last glorious morsel at once. Glenna happily complied, pausing only long enough to pour more wine or to wait for an end to the men's shouts downstairs. Finally, she got to her last and most important part. "Cowan suggests we have a feast and invite the Haldane."

"But is it wise?" Steppen asked. "If Lorna truly prefers Cowan, then she will be heartsick to see him court a Haldane."

Jonrose disagreed. "It is kinder to let her see it now than later after he has taken Lasha to wife and brought her home."

Glenna nodded, "True and if she knows now, perhaps it is not too late for Lorna to let Cowan know how she feels. It would not be the first time a lad changed his mind when he learned there were more possibilities."

It was settled then. The women would talk Neil into having a feast and inviting the Haldane. That meant there were plans to be made and they got right down to business. They talked about the food they would serve, the dancing, the singing and the sports the men liked to partake in. It had been a while since the woman had anything that exciting to do and all three of them were delighted.

Suddenly, they heard Ben shouting downstairs "Alison lives!"

Ben ran back out the door, got half way across the courtyard, turned and ran back. "It's a laddie!"

CHAPTER V

When he awoke, Cowan was still thinking about Lasha and quickly decided to do his hunting south of the MacGreagor village again. By noon, he was doing much less hunting and a lot more watching. He watched the Haldane hunters leave, watched other men and women tend the animals and sat on a log to watch the children play, but there was no sign of Lasha. At least there wasn't any yelling from inside the Keep either. Cowan bet it would not last much longer.

At length, Lasha came outside.

Earlier, Cowan noticed one of the men tie a horse in the courtyard near the Keep but he was surprised when Lasha walked to it, loaded her sack on its back, stepped up on a nearby log and then mounted. That she could ride a horse did not surprise him, but that she rode down the northern end of the Haldane valley alone did. As quickly as he could, he mounted and followed her.

He told himself he needed to protect her but he wanted to watch her as well. Where did a woman like Lasha go all alone and what did she think about? A little while later, she answered his first question.

Lasha halted, dismounted and walked to a rock large enough for her to sit on at the edge of the loch. As lakes go, it was small and just right for the dozen or so swans that floated on the top. She settled herself and wondered how long it would be before the MacGreagor hunter let her know he was there. Men like to think they are not easy to detect in the forest, she was aware, but somehow she knew he was near. She could not explain it, but she felt it all morning and when she looked more diligently than she normally would have, she spotted him following her.

That was one reason she stopped. The other was to watch the swans. The pure white swans were beautiful and when they were not up-ending to search for tasty morsels of submerged plants, they floated on top rubbing their beaks and the base of their long necks together as though they were hopelessly in love. She wanted to be in love like that someday.

That made her think of Sionn and she could not help but frown. She had no feeling whatsoever for the man and could not imagine loving him. But her brother once said women fall in love after marriage. He knew it to be true because their parents were promised and did not even meet until their wedding day. Yet their mother grew to love their father very much.

Lasha was not convinced.

For most of her ordinary day, she was bored with little to do and no one who really needed her. She wanted a home and family of her own, but not if it meant never knowing how it felt to be in love. What foolishness is this, she thought. Marriage to Sionn was a given and there was little she could do about it. For a moment she wondered if marriage to a man she had never seen before might be preferred over giving herself to a man she knew she did not love. Lasha sighed.

"Are you unwell?"

She knew he was there, but not this close and his voice startled her. She caught her breath, quickly turned and then breathed easier. "Oh good, you have saved me."

"From what?"

"From having to ride all the way to the MacGreagor hold." He looked befuddled, which made her smile, "To return your plaid. It is in my sack."

At last, she let him see her dimples and it pleased him very much. "Then I am glad to save you the trouble." He spotted a blue pebble in the dirt, leaned down and picked it up. Cowan made his way over the larger rocks until he could kneel down and wash it in the water. "I have a nephew who will be very pleased to have this rock, it is almost perfectly round."

"How old is he?"

"Not yet eight. He will begin warrior training soon." Cowan looked the pebble over once more and then slipped it into the small, cloth sack tied to his belt."

"All laddies dream of being mighty warriors."

"And all lassies dream of being queens." He hoped she would ask him to sit, but she did not, so he retraced his steps away from the loch and then put one foot up on a small rock and remained standing.

Lasha giggled. "I too dreamed of being the queen. Shall I confess how disappointed I was when I learned there was only one King of Scotland and he already had a wife?"

Cowan chuckled. "I can see how that might be upsetting. Fortunately for little boys, the clans need all the warriors they can get." She turned away to watch the swans and he remained quiet for a little while, although he was watching her more than the swans. "What were you thinking about before I came?"

She did not truly want to tell him, but she could not think of a good lie either. "If you must know, I was thinking about the lad I will marry."

"I see. Are you betrothed?"

"Nay, not yet."

He pretended to look back to check on the horses so she could not see how pleased he was to hear it. "I believe my laird is thinking of having a feast to which the Haldanes will be invited. Do you think your brother will accept?"

Lasha puffed her cheeks and slowly let the air out. "I do not know. He took your suggestion, put Ena out and it has been blissfully quiet all day. I have you to thank for that."

"You are quite welcome. Tell me, would you have come all the way to the MacGreagor hold alone just to bring back my plaid?" When she reached out her hand, he took it and helped her up. Then he held on to it as she made her way over the rocks toward the horses.

Once more his touch mystified her and suddenly she was determined -- as soon as she could find him, she fully intended to touch Sionn just to see if she found him just a perplexing."

"Lasha?"

"What? Oh, do forgive me, I was thinking of something else."

"Something I can help with?"

She giggled, "You have done quite enough." She did not mean to say that and found herself trying to quickly recover. "After all, you found Laird Haldane's son and returned him. I could never ask you to do more than that."

Cowan pretended to pout. "I am deeply disappointed."

"You are?"

She looked genuinely concerned so he smiled to ease her mind. "All lads like to think they can be of some help to a lass."

"That is odd. I was thinking the same thing before you came. I want a home of my own and a family who needs me. Being needed is very important, do you agree?"

"I do. Are you unhappy living with your brother...aside from having to endure his wife, I mean."

"Not unhappy particularly. I love my brother very much, but he does not need me. His wife does not need me, the laddie does not need me and ..."

"Being needed is very important."

"Aye." She turned, pulled her sack off her horse and opened it. Then she reached inside and pulled out his clean plaid. "It is washed. I hope it is clean enough."

He was sure it was, he'd watched her wash it for the better part of an hour the day before. Still, he unfolded part of it, gave it a good look and then nodded. "I find it be very clean indeed."

She was pleased, he was pleased and they seemed to run out of things to say, but he did not want to leave and she did not want him to. Instead, she wanted to touch his face. She knew she should not, but before she realized what she was doing the inside of her hand was flat against his cheek. Suddenly horrified, she quickly jerked it away. "I am...I did not mean..."

But he didn't move. Instead, he took hold of her hand and put it back on his face. He watched her eyes, slowly put his arm around her waist and gently pulled. She did not resist, yet she seemed stiff and uncertain so he did nothing more. Instead, he waited and then as he hoped, she took a small step closer and put her head and both her hands on his chest. Her face was turned away from his, but Cowan did not mind. He closed his eyes, wrapped his other arm around her and memorized the feel of her in his arms. She was not yet completely relaxed and so he put his cheek against the top of her head and again he waited.

The only other man who had ever held her that close was her brother and while his embrace was comforting, it was nothing like… "What is your name?"

"I am Cowan MacGreagor."

She felt him tighten his arms a little more and welcomed it. Never had she felt anything so glorious. "This is wrong, is it not?"

"It is not wrong unless you are betrothed and you said you were not."

She pulled away just enough to look up at him. "I did not lie. It is just that…"

"It is just that you like being in my arms and therefore we must be doing something wrong?"

"Aye. If you tell me it is not wrong, I will believe you."

"It is not wrong."

She smiled, put her head back against his chest and closed her eyes. She knew if she lifted her head again, he would kiss her, but she was not ready for that. From the time she was little she watched her brother kiss his wife. At first it was disgusting but as she got older, she studied it and each time his wife lifted her face to him, he kissed her. It was like a signal of some sort. Therefore, she knew not to do that. On the other hand, she wondered what it might be like if…"

"Lasha."

Suddenly uncertain what she really wanted, she could not risk lifting her face to him. "What?"

He felt her stiffen, was afraid he frightened her and let go. "I would like very much to stay, but I am expected to do a little hunting."

She grinned. "Of course." She took a step back and lowered her head.

But he could not bear to leave her like that. He put a finger under her chin and lifted her face. Just as she had the day before, he softly kissed her lips. "It is not wrong." With that, he mounted his horse and rode north.

CHAPTER VI

Lasha watched him go and then made her way back to the edge of the loch. She sat back down, watched the swans and tried to understand what was happening to her. Cowan…his name was Cowan and he said touching him was not wrong, but he did not know about Sionn. Earlier, she was determined to see if Sionn's touch made her feel the same, but now she could not bear to lose the feel of Cowan's arms so soon. Therefore, it *was* wrong and it was all her fault. If she had not kissed Cowan that first day her head would not be filled with thoughts of him and she could marry Sionn without ever knowing the difference. If only she had not kissed Cowan. Cowan…his name was Cowan MacGreagor and she feared she was already hopelessly in love with him.

Lasha stayed by the loch as long as she dared and then rode home. Suddenly she remembered what Cowan told her about the feast and was anxious to tell her brother, but life was never simple and thoughts of normal things were easily set aside. Ena forgot herself and started yelling again.

This time when the Haldane bent over to grab his wife behind the knees, she wiggled free of his grasp. However, instead of chasing her around the room, he calmly walked to the table, picked up a challis filled with water, turned and threw it in her face. He set it down and while Ena was recovering from her shock, he bent down, grabbed her behind the knees and slung her over his shoulder. He paused just long enough for Lasha to open the door, carried her out and set her down in the middle of the courtyard.

It was then that he noticed the people had gathered to watch. Ena was quite a sight sitting in the dirt with water dripping from her hair down her face, and they looked as if they wanted to laugh. But she was, after all, their mistress. "You may laugh if you wish. She has laughed at you often enough."

Ena frowned, narrowed her eyes and opened her mouth determined to give her husband a piece of her mind, but just then she noticed not one, but two men bringing buckets of water to their laird.

"Ena, there will be no more of your yelling."

Her husband looked determined, his sister looked determined, the whole clan looked determined and even her toddler son had his hands on his hips glaring at her. "Well I…"

"Promise you will not yell and you can come back in."

It took a great deal of courage for Ena to swallow her pride and submit to her husband's demands, but sitting in the dirt with people staring at her was not to her liking either. "Oh very well then, I will stop yelling but…"

"But what, my love, what do you want?"

"I want you to listen to me occasionally. I only yell because you do not hear me?"

He offered her his hand, "I assure you, in these many years I have heard every word and I would answer, should you ever stop talking long enough for me to get a word or two said."

With his help, Ena pulled herself up and then brushed off the back of her skirt.

The whole time, Lasha had not really been listening. She spotted Sionn near the back of the crowd and watched him instead. She watched him laugh at Ena, watched him roll his eyes at something Ena said and she watched him glance back to see if his horse was where it should be. But not once did he look at her. Again she caught herself mentally comparing the two men and again she reminded herself nothing good could come of that. Sionn would lose on every score and she had not even given him the opportunity to compete.

She thought about touching Sionn, but it occurred to her he would see her touch as encouragement. On the other hand, what if his touch was distasteful? Shouldn't she know that before she agreed to marry him? Finally, Sionn looked at her. By then, everyone else including her brother and his wife had gone home and she was standing there alone watching him. She wondered if he would walk away, but he came to her instead.

"Will you walk with me?"

Lasha nodded knowing full well by the time they returned the whole clan would have them betrothed if not already married. They might not be wrong, she reasoned and although she could not think of anything to say, she fell into step beside him.

He did not seem to know what to say either, which soon annoyed her. They were half way down the small valley when she finally broke the silence, "What do you want?"

Sionn was taken aback by her question and stopped to stare at her, "What?"

"I mean, what do you want in a wife?"

"Oh, I do not know, the usual I suppose. I need a wife to give me children."

"And I need a husband to give me children."

He smiled, "Unless you have thought of another way."

This conversation was not at all going where she wanted it to. "But having children is not all there is to marriage. What kind of woman do you want to spend your days with? Should she be good humored, quiet, prone to argue…what?"

"Lasha, I hardly see the point of this discussion. I must marry you and you must marry me. Neither of us has a choice in the matter."

This time is was Lasha who was stunned. She had not realized Sionn felt as trapped as she did. She took a deep breath and slowly let it out. "I know." She wanted him to take her in his arms and let her know it would be all right, but he did not so she started to walk again. "Will we be happy or will we hate each other, do you think?"

"I am a good hunter and you will never go hungry or without skins for warmth in winter. But I cannot promise you happiness. I will try, but I cannot promise it."

His honesty was something she always admired about him and she was pleased with it now. "Why did you ask me to marry you now? I mean we have known each other since birth. Why not a week ago or even last year?"

Sionn studied her eyes for a moment. "I believed there was time still. I hoped to build you a fine cottage with everything new and clean. But…."

"But what?"

"You kissed the MacGreagor."

She quickly lowered her gaze. "I only meant to thank him."

"Aye, but I do not believe he understood that. I fear he will tempt you away and I will have to…"

"You will have to marry Doileag?"

He returned her grin. "She might be quite handsome when she is grown, but right now."

"It is possible she will *not* be quite handsome when she is grown too."

"Aye, there is that. Married to you will at least allow me to hope for daughters with your very pleasing dimples."

"Good heavens, you have never complimented me before. I am quite charmed."

Sionn held out his hand and waited for her to take it. "I admit I have been remiss. I thought there was still time, you see."

Lasha took his hand. She did not feel excitement in his touch but neither was she repulsed and she began to consider her brother might be right -- a woman can fall in love after marriage -- particularly with a man who remembers to compliment her occasionally.

*

Cowan wanted nothing more than to go back the next day to see if Lasha was at the loch watching the swans. But he had not produced much food for the clan in two days and soon some of the other men would suspect. If a man who loved the thrill of the hunt was distracted it could only mean one thing -- his mind was on a woman instead.

As hard as it was, Cowan stayed away for one complete day, hunted and brought one deer and two rabbits to the clan. It was enough to wave off their suspicions at least for a while.

On the second day, he could not wait to ride into the forest and make his way to the loch. He found her just as he hoped on the same rock, but this time the sight of her took his breath away. She had taken the ties out of her braids and was combing her silky, waist length hair with her fingers. Every once in a while, the breeze lifted loose strands and the sun turned them to a golden shade of brown.

CHAPTER VII

This time she heard him coming and turned just before he reached her. Lasha wanted to jump up and run to him. Her heart ached to be in his arms again, but there was something to be said and she'd spent the previous two days practicing to say it.

He hoped she might be happy to see him, but when he approached, she did not smile. "What is it?"

"Will you sit with me?" She watched his nod and then waited for him to find a rock and sit down not far from her. Instead of talking to him, she turned to watch the swans. She thought she had all the right words chosen, but with him so close, she could not remember what they were.

"Has someone died?"

She glanced at him and then quickly looked away. "Nay, it is not quite *that* serious."

"What then?"

"I am a Haldane." When he started to comment, she held up her hand to stop him. "In ancient times, my ancestor lived under a harsh and cruel laird whom he detested. He convinced other families to join him in making a new clan. They slipped away in the night, found this land and were very happy for about a year. But the men the Haldane took with him were Laird Clarion's strongest and best warriors. As a result, the Clarions lost their land in a war with another clan. They blamed Laird Haldane, sought him out and killed all but three members of his family. From these three, we have grown and it is our solemn vow to keep the clan together in memory of our ancestor. It is fitting, proper and good. Do you not agree?"

Cowan suspected there was some hidden meaning in her story and was hesitant, but at length he nodded. "Why do you tell me this?"

"Because we cannot honor his memory if our women marry outside our clan."

He felt as though an arrow had pierced his heart and tried desperately to hide his pain by turning and pretending to watch the swans. He ran his fingers through his hair and tried to think of some reasonable argument. "Have you already made your pledge?"

She took a deep breath and closed her eyes. "Not yet, but I can put him off no longer. He is a good lad; he will not hurt me."

"Do you love him?"

It was the question she feared most and she fully intended to say she did, but a tear rolled down her cheek. She brushed it away and instead of saying yes, she said nothing at all.

"Lasha, I…"

"Try to understand, you are the forbidden fruit. To love you would be to hurt my brother and my clan. I cannot do that."

"There is little I can say, then." He stood back up and offered her his hand. For a long moment, she stared at it and then at last, her hand was in his. Suddenly, she was in his arms once more, his lips were on hers and she was returning his passion with her own.

He held her in his embrace until Lasha finally pulled away. "Will you change your mind?"

"Nay."

He held both her hands and looked into her eyes. "If he hurts you…if ever you should need me, tie a cloth around at tree at the edge of this clearing and I will come to you."

She reluctantly pulled her hands away, "I will not have you coming here every day to look for a cloth. Knowing you are so close and not being able to be with you would make me daft in a fortnight."

At least at that he could smile, "It would not take me nearly as long."

Lasha put a finger to his lips. "Promise you will not come back. I must forget you and you must be free to find another love. Please, please, promise you will not come back."

Cowan did not promise. Instead, he took her in his arms once more, kissed her hard, walked away and then mounted his horse. Just before he left, he said, "Do you believe your ancestor truly wanted you to be miserable for his sake?"

She thought about that briefly, watched him go and in just a few moments, he disappeared into the forest. He was gone, she loved him and being in his arms for such a short time was not enough. Lasha couldn't help herself. She sunk to her knees and wept. Nothing short of the death of her father had hurt so much as this.

*

On the other side of the loch, Sionn watched it all. He saw the MacGreagor leave and watched Lasha weeping. But instead of going to her or even chasing after the MacGreagor as most men would have, he rode back to the village, brushed his horse dry and then put him out to pasture.

Each day Lasha went to the loch to watch the swans. She wavered between hoping Cowan would come and praying he would not. He stayed away and each time she left the loch without seeing him, she hurt yet again.

In the evenings, she walked with Sionn and tried to convince herself he was the right husband. She was learning to like him well enough, she just did not love him…not the way she loved Cowan. Sionn held her finally, on the evening of the third day and she let him kiss her.

There was no fire or passion. It was just a kiss.

Maybe the fire and the passion would come later but she was not holding out much hope. Sionn did not seem any more pleased with the kiss than she was and once she was back in her little room, she sat on the bed, pulled her knees up under her chin and wept. Life had suddenly become cruel and unforgiving.

*

By midmorning of the fourth day everything changed. One of the Haldane men shouted something about MacGreagors and everyone rushed to the courtyard to watch. Lasha was amazed to see Cowan and two other men riding their horses down the hillside. At first Laird Haldane's men kept their hands on the handle of their swords prepared to fight, but their laird saw nothing threatening and waved his hand to ease them. Then he stood in the middle of the courtyard and waited.

The MacGreagors did not dismount and it was Cowan who spoke. "Laird MacGreagor and his wife wish the company of you and all your followers two days next at our village for a feast. Will you come?" He tried not to, but he could not help looking at Lasha. Then he noticed the man standing behind her and thought he saw a hint of displeasure. This had to be the man Lasha planned to marry and to avoid trouble; Cowan quickly looked away.

"All of us?" asked Laird Haldane, "We can hardly leave the place with no protection. We do not have much, but what we have we cannot live without."

"My laird said to offer guards for your village. He wants very much for all the Haldanes to know not to fear us."

Ena came out of the Keep and put her arm around her husband. "I think it is a fine idea. I long to hear all the gossip first hand for a change, instead of third or fourth."

"Do you my dear?" He kissed her forehead and then smiled at Cowan. "We accept."

Cowan dared to glace at Lasha again and was surprised to find both she and the man behind her smiling. Perhaps he was not the man she intended to marry after all. "I will tell Laird MacGreagor to expect you."

*

Everyone was excited, not just because the MacGreagors were preparing for a feast, but because two more women had given birth the night before and survived. Perhaps the curse was lifted, if indeed there was a curse.

The weather was very good, to the relief of them all and the large courtyard was the perfect place to feed so many. The women cooked, the men carried tables and chairs outside and set up the games of skill in the field where they normally practiced their warrior skills. Other men tended the meat of three deer that had been slow cooking in the pits for two days, and the children raced around until their parents sent them off to play somewhere else.

The air smelled of burning wood one minute and fresh flowers the next with an occasional breeze that blew in from the direction of the river. Finally, there was nothing left to do but wait for their guests and the three men, Neil, Walrick and Gelson were happy to just stand next to their wives in the courtyard and enjoy the people.

Walrick had been acting odd all morning and suddenly could not contain his news a moment longer, "Steppen is with child at last."

Glenna and Jonrose shrieked with joy while the men slapped Walrick on the back. Neil especially grinned. He thought he already saw beads of sweat on Walrick's brow and he was going to enjoy every moment of Walrick's worry. After all the congratulations were said, Neil turned his attention back to the others. Thomas and Julia were busy taunting each other and entertaining their friends.

Ralin and Taral set their bowls of vegetables on the table and then went to Neil. Together they curtsied and laughed when Neil rolled his eyes. They claimed it had been so long since they curtsied, they needed the practice before Laird Haldane arrived. Soon, the other women came to stand in front of him, one by one curtsying and grinning. Glorie was the first, having finally been allowed back in Glenna's good graces. Then came Jessup, Kadick and Mayze, Catlin and Greer, Bethia and Alison, Edana and Slava, Clare and Dolee, and the last to stand before him was a beautiful young woman with deep dimples the likes of which Neil had never seen before.

"I am Lasha Haldane." Her curtsey was gracious and her smile was genuine.

Neil leaned closer to Glenna but he spoke loud enough for everyone to hear, "My dear, are you quite certain I am married?"

Glenna winked at Lasha and then gritted her teeth. "Until death, which might be sooner than you think."

Everyone laughed and Neil offered his hand to help Lasha stand. "You are very pleasing to the eye, you are aware."

Lasha was not used to such words and blushed. Soon she managed to get herself out of the spotlight and away from where her brother and her sister-in-law were being greeted. When she thought it was safe, she looked for him.

There were so many more MacGreagors than she realized and she did not want to be obvious, so she slowly looked at each one. She smiled at the women, nodded to the men and then looked at the next couple. Suddenly a MacGreagor woman was standing right in front of her.

CHAPTER VIII

Aleen was the youngest of the nine sisters and over the months, she had grown to be almost as tall as Lasha. She cupped her hands and whispered in Lasha's ear. "Come with me, I want you to meet my friend, Lorna." Lasha hardly had a choice. Aleen had a firm grip on her arm and was pulling her down a deserted path between the cottages. Faster and faster, she pulled until they reached a certain cottage, rounded the corner and abruptly stopped. There, half hidden by a bush was Sionn. His arms were wrapped around a MacGreagor woman, he was kissing her passionately and Lasha could do nothing but stare at the two of them.

He suddenly noticed she was there, quickly moved away from the woman and hung his head.

Aleen grabbed Lasha's arm once more to get her attention. "This is my friend, Lorna and she loves Sionn. He loves her too, only…"

Behind them, it was Cowan who interrupted. "Only Sionn and Lasha must marry within their own clan."

Sionn again lowered his eyes. "I am so sorry, Lasha, I did not mean for you to ever find out."

Lorna began to cry which made Lasha quickly go to her. "If you cry, then I will cry and if someone sees us, they will think the men have done something awful. She took out her cloth and wiped Lorna's tears away. Lasha guessed the girl was not yet sixteen and overwhelmed with being in love and then being told marriage to Sionn was out of the question. Lasha felt sorrier for her than she did for herself. She tried to comfort the lass with a smile and then turned her attention to Sionn, "You need not feel such shame, you are not the only one who has…"

"I know, I saw you."

"You saw me kiss the MacGreagor? And you were not angry?"

"How can I be angry? It is clear you love him and besides, all I can think about is Lorna. We have been meeting in the woods nearly every day."

Lasha walked back to stand next to Cowan. "I fear we are all destined to be unhappy for the rest of our lives."

"There must be something we can do," mumbled Sionn.

Emotionally exhausted, Lasha closed her eyes and rubbed her brow. "Cowan is right, our ancestor could not have wanted so many of us to be miserable for his sake. But making my brother understand that will be impossible. He has declared I marry a Haldane and I must obey him." The alarmed look on Cowan's face and the way the color drained out of Sionn's caused Lasha to catch her breath. "Is my brother standing behind me?"

Sionn shook his head, "Nay, it is Laird MacGreagor."

Lasha slowly turned to face him. "Have you been there long?"

"Long enough," he answered and then directed his next remark to Sionn. "If you do not take Lasha back, her brother will soon come looking for her."

*

They ate, danced to the music of the flute, played games, laughed and the clans got to know each other. Some of the Haldane men were quite skilled at the games which impressed the MacGreagors. But two MacGreagors and two Haldanes were exceedingly unhappy.

Cowan and Lorna MacGreagor sat together all the way across the courtyard from Lasha and Sionn Haldane. They exchanged sad glances, whispered something to the one they sat next to occasionally and tried to enjoy the entertainment. But it was evident they thought of nothing but trying to find an answer to their very complicated and unthinkable problem.

Occasionally, Ena's voice got a little loud and all the Haldanes prayed she would not embarrass them, but soon enough she quieted. Ena, it seemed, had been tamed.

Seated at the table in a row facing the people, the two lairds and their wives finished eating and it was Haldane who finally began the conversation. "A fine feast, MacGreagor, a fine feast indeed. But I have one complaint?"

Neil looked horrified, "What might that be?"

"Your wife sits on the other side of you, my wife sits on the other side of me and my wife cannot get her fill of gossip that way."

Neil smiled and before he could ask, Glenna got up. She was thrilled, kissed her husband, beamed at Laird Haldane and then took Ena's hand. "I have so much to tell it will likely take all night. Come with me." Soon the two excited women disappeared inside the MacGreagor keep.

The Haldane leaned just a little closer to Neil, "I believe my wife will be in gossip heaven for quite some time after we leave. I shall invite you to our home, but frankly, we cannot feed so many. Perhaps…"

"I often prefer smaller numbers anyway."

"Good."

Neil did not know the man and could not guess his reaction to interference in family matters, but he had to try. "I hear tell you love your wife."

"Cannot imagine a world without her, though there are days I regret having met her."

Neil thought about all the stories he heard about Ena and smiled. He refilled Haldane's empty goblet and then pointed across the courtyard. "Do you see that lad and that lass?"

"Aye, the lass is my sister. She will soon marry the lad with her."

"Aye, but your sister does not love him."

"Perhaps not, but she will in time." Haldane saw the doubt in Neil's eyes and took a moment to look once more at the young couple. He had not noticed before, but each looked gloomy. "They are quite beside themselves, I see. Still, it will pass. Lasha is a good lass and she will do her duty."

"Aye, but the lad she is with does not love her either."

"But..."

Neil quickly interrupted and pointed to the other side of the courtyard. "And do you see that lad and that lass?"

"Aye."

"That is the lad who loves your sister and with him is the lass who loves Sionn."

"I see." At first Haldane seemed a little put out, but he took the time to closely study each couple.

"If I had a sister, I would want her to know the kind of love I have for my wife."

"They are young; they will learn to love each other."

"And if they do not? It would indeed be a high price to pay simply to give her clan children."

"MacGreagor, we are a small clan. The loss of even one lass can decrease our growth by quite a number of children."

"Aye, but Lorna MacGreagor would be more than pleased to supply you with all the children she can manage. All you need do is bless her marriage to Sionn instead of your sister." Neil decided he had said quite enough, folded his arms and remembered to breathe.

It was a new avenue of thinking suddenly open to the Haldane. Some months back he considered letting his men intermarry with the Kennedys, but everyone hated the Kennedys and they would want an alliance he was unwilling to give. He did not trust the other clans either especially after Laird Graham was trampled by his horse and now there was a new laird. Who knew what might become of that clan? It took so little to turn some men in to beasts these days it seemed. But just now he had a new possibility. He could consider intermarriage with the MacGreagors.

"Have you more lasses in mind for my lads? I have two and perhaps three in want of a wife."

Neil was relieved. A question…any question at all meant Haldane was actually giving the idea careful consideration. "I know of no reason not to let your men find wives among the MacGreagors." Neil took a sip of wine, although he had already drank more than he cared to. "Of course there is still the situation with your sister. It is our Cowan she loves and I believe you know him. He rescued your son."

Haldane looked at Cowan for a long moment, abruptly stood up and when he did, everyone noticed and got quiet. "Lasha, come here!"

Her brother never yelled and Lasha was immediately alarmed. So was Cowan who quickly went to her side. She eyed her brother's glower for a moment and then cautiously walked between the people until she stood face to face with him. By then, Neil was also standing. Lasha dared not say a word and by the fierce look on her brother's face, she was grateful there was a table between them.

Haldane glared at Cowan for a moment, but when the young man did not look away, it impressed him. Then he glared at his sister until he was reminded how much she looked like their departed mother. "Do you love Sionn?"

Lasha felt guilty for saying it and stared down at the tabletop. "Nay, I do not."

The Haldane looked for Sionn in the crowd and was surprised to find him not far away holding the hand of the woman Neil pointed out earlier. "Sionn, do you love my sister?"

He too bowed his head, "Nay, I do not."

"Has Lasha already agreed to marry you?"

"Nay, she has not yet given me an answer," said Sionn.

This time Haldane narrowed his eyes and turned his glare back on Cowan. "Cowan MacGreagor, have you kissed my sister?"

Cowan was confused for a moment. Of course he kissed her, or rather she kissed him, and Haldane was witness to it. Finally realizing what the man was up to, Cowan nodded, "I confess I have."

Haldane let his eyes roll back in his head as though he was thoroughly disgusted. "Someone find the priest! Any lad who kisses my sister must marry her and we've no time to waste. He quickly turned to look at Neil, "Do you agree?"

"I do indeed."

Cowan drew Lasha into his arms and when he kissed her full on the mouth neither one of them noticed the cheers of the crowd.

*

They did not hold just one wedding that evening, but two -- Lasha and Cowan became husband and wife first and then the priest married Sionn and Lorna. The priest was so long winded, the elder Cobb fell asleep twice during the ceremonies. Both clans made merry long into the night, so long in fact, the Haldanes stayed the night, which gave Glenna and Ena even more time to gossip.

In the morning, life began anew. The rooster crowed, the swans landed on the loch and the animals left the warmth of their forest beds to search for a morning meal. The hearths were lit, the babies were fed and before Ben went to his bed after a long night of caring for the livestock, he reported two new colts.

And Lasha woke up in the home she always dreamed of and in the arms of the man she loved.

---The End---

Coming Soon – Book 3 in the Viking series.

MORE MARTI TALBOTT BOOKS

Marti Talbott's Highlander Series: books 1 – 5 are short stories that follow the MacGreagor clan through two generations. They are followed by:

Betrothed, Book 6

The Golden Sword, Book 7

Abducted, Book 8

A Time of Madness, Book 9

Triplets, Book 10

Secrets, Book 11

Choices, Book 12

Ill-Fated Love Book 13

The Other Side of the River, Book 14

The Viking Series:

The Viking, Book 1 explains how the clan came into being.

The Viking's Daughter, Book 2

Book 3 is coming soon.

Marblestone Mansion (Scandalous Duchess Series) follows the MacGreagor clan into Colorado's early 20th century. There are currently 10 books in this series.

The Jackie Harlan Mysteries

Seattle Quake 9.2, Book 1

Missing Heiress, Book 2

Greed and a Mistress, Book 3

The Carson Series

The Promise, Book 1

Broken Pledge, Book 2

Talk to Marti on Facebook at:

https://www.facebook.com/marti.talbott

Sign up to be notified when new books are published at:

http://www.martitalbott.com